By the sa

Tales of Peril a

Each book a series of short stories, ancient and modern, in locations around the world.
They include a few early-life glimpses of George Goode.

Pebbles on the Shore
One Scoop or Two?
Lucky Dip
Hook, Line and Sinker
Tapestry Tangles

Cornish Conundrums

Full-length crime stories, featuring industrial mathematician George Gilbert (née Goode) and friends, stemming from her projects in different parts of Cornwall.

Doom Watch
Slate Expectations
Looe's Connections
Tunnel Vision
Twisted Limelight
Forever Mine:
Crown Dual
Unsettled Score
Brush with Death
Beyond Reach

David Burnell comes from York. He studied maths at Cambridge and went on to teach it to sixth formers in West Africa. After one of his students came back from Kumasi University to replace him, he returned to the UK and applied maths to management problems in health, coal mining and lastly the water industry. Devising daily schedules for the many pumps on the new London Ring Main was one major project. Narrowing uncertainty on leakage was another. His team won awards from the British Computer Society and the Operational Research Society. On "retiring" he completed a PhD at Lancaster University on what really happened to London's water.

He and his wife split their time between Berkshire and North Cornwall. They have four grown-up children.

BLACK HOLE, SILVER LINING

Tales of Peril and Predicament

David Burnell

Skein Books

BLACK HOLE, SILVER LINING

Published by Skein Books, 88, Woodcote Rd, Caversham, Reading, UK

First edition: November 2022.

ISBN: 9798364094278

The front cover shows a storm-threatened view over the Atlantic at North Cornwall, with a sliver of light shining through. The cover background is a local golf course. Thanks to my wife, Marion, for the front photograph; and also for the author photo on the back cover.

FOREWORD

Several of these stories started from the Thames Valley Writers Circle. "Flight from Mariupol" won our 2022 competition, as assessed by top short-story author Iain Pattison.

Other new characters include Miles and Sally Henderson, contrasting painters and decorators. One offers expertise on finance, the other contributes all sorts of flair.

I've also invented another antique dealer, who goes by the name of Lovejoy.

This book includes several problems for Greg and Laurie, enthusiastic but modest golfers.

It also outlines the start of the relationship between George Goode and Mark Gilbert. George will be well-known to readers of my full-length Cornish Conundrums.

There is also another episode for Lauren Shaw, a West Indian police officer in a largely white man's world.

Finally there is a further episode from the tangled aftermath of the Russian invasion.

A varied set of Tales of Peril and Predicament. Fourteen are set in the present day, the remainder in the twentieth century. All but two are set in Britain.

The collection includes only one Black Hole but several with Silver Linings. I hope you enjoy the read.

CONTENTS

Tales of Peril and Predicament

1. FLIGHT FROM MARIUPOL

The scene was horrific. Not just the detritus of battle – you'd expect that in any war. Nor the smashed production units – all that was left of what had been the largest steel plant in Europe. Not even the repeatedly bombed hospital, once the pride of Mariupol. What finally dented my apathy to the aftermath of war was when I saw the primary school targeted by heavy shelling: over fifty children, plus dozens of adults, cruelly torn into thousands of bloody pieces. Wars had consequences; and not just for those taking an active part.

I was a war correspondent: Annastasia Kozlov. You won't have heard of me. Not much of a job but there wasn't much choice. I'd learned about kit and tactics, not bothered about moral choices. War was a way of staying safe in a hostile world, even if it sometimes meant a pre-emptive strike. It was up to leaders to make choices; and armies to make them happen.

Which meant that if I was now to change – from being a detached observer of a brutal war to a full-blooded opponent – I had somehow to reach my leaders and cause them to change their minds.

As I pondered, the caustic chatter of the soldiers stung me for the first time. How could anyone be so callous and uncaring? Didn't these men have partners and children of their own? Had military life turned them from men into robots?

'Got the details, Anna?' asked the sergeant. 'We're heading for the tunnels now. That's where the animals are hiding.' Though he didn't use such polite words. Or sound so calm.

'I'm going back to base,' I replied, 'post our successes so far.' I had enough acting skills to cover my real feelings. He wasn't interested in me, anyway. So it was that I started my long journey home.

The best way to travel was by bus. I couldn't afford the train fare; or risk heavy security checks. Buses were checked on too, of course, but more lightly - or so I'd been told.

It was 800 miles to the capital. I was in reporting gear: dark jumper, black jeans and a reporter's pass. It would have to do. Three hours later I was on the rear seat of a night coach heading for the capital. As we set off, I saw an official, quizzing passengers from the front. He looked a thug. I had perhaps twenty minutes to make up a convincing reason for my journey away from the war zone.

'*I'm hoping to see the President. Tell him the reality of war is murdered children. Persuade him to try a different approach.*' I couldn't say that, anyway. I'd be dropped off at the first police station for prolonged interrogation. The task suddenly seemed enormous. I hadn't thought this hard, outside the box, in my whole life.

As the Official worked slowly down the coach, my mind froze: I had nothing to say, was heading for disaster. Then he reached a vagabond slumped two seats in front of me, high on alcohol or drugs; and the confrontation began.

The Official spoke calmly but the man wasn't having it and swore back ferociously. He'd obviously spent time in the forces. Inside a minute the two were punching away, as hard as any troops I'd met in Mariupol. The rest of us kept back as far as we could. Soon the din reached the driver. One look in his mirror and the coach screeched to a halt. Not to separate the protagonists, but to call the police.

Twenty minutes later both men had been hauled away and our journey resumed. Phew. I'd escaped scrutiny but I badly needed a plan. Or perhaps a collaborator?

As we continued, we kept passing posters about the forth-coming Mayday Parade, recalling the historic victory over the Nazis. All carried pictures of the President and his exhortations to continue the battle in Ukraine, where, it appeared, "victory was almost in sight". It occurred to me: the Parade would be one event where he was guaranteed to be found.

Which in turn brought me to my brother, Artur. He had confessed, privately, that he'd be in the Parade too. Did he know what was really going on in Ukraine? Was he amenable to being told?

It was dark by now and the coach rumbled on. We'd be in Moscow just before dawn. But how would I get to my brother, inside his airbase? I was an accredited war reporter, but how would I even get in? Though this seemed easier than trying to reach the President. I fell into a troubled sleep as I wrestled with ideas, one wilder than another.

The jolt woke me as we reached the Moscow coach station. It was a five kilometre walk to my tiny apartment, but I'd done it before. Now the stark contrast between the culture here and the carnage I'd left behind in Mariupol brought me almost to tears.

It was as I walked through the downtown suburb that I was struck. Not by an idea, but by the Deliveroo delivery boy as he pedalled fiercely round the corner, almost knocking me over.

'Hey, watch it,' I cried.

He turned to see the damage. Which in turn cause him to keel over and fall off, as his bike hit the kerb. At least he'd a sense of humour; he was still grinning as I walked over to check he was alright.

'I'm really sorry, miss.'

I was about to leave him and go on my way when I noticed his emerald-green, hooded uniform, so ubiquitous around Moscow that it was almost invisible.

'Tell you what,' I said. 'You can scarper, provided you hand over your uniform and bike. I'll buy them off you. What are they worth?'

He was a shrewd youngster. No doubt he'd make up some story to account for the loss. We agreed a price, I handed it over and we parted, me now in the green suit and on wheels. With a bit of luck I might have found a way of getting through to my brother.

Artur's base was on the far side of Moscow, but now I was mobile. It was after breakfast by the time I reached the camp, a good time for delivery. More emerald-green suits were waiting; we were all waved through the security gate with a perfunctory nod.

I knew where to find Artur's quarters, but was he in? I knocked optimistically.

The door opened, he saw the green suit and blinked. 'Did I order something?'

'Can I come in?' My whisper alerted him; he inspected me carefully.

'Anna! Well, this is a surprise. That's one way to sidestep security, I suppose. Aren't you meant to be reporting on our lads' heroic successes in Ukraine?'

It was a welcome, anyway. I followed him inside and sat down. 'I couldn't do it any more, Artur. Our leaders have told us a pack of lies. And led us into daily war crimes. I myself saw a school shelled to oblivion, with the children still inside – all in tiny pieces. Destroyed by our own tanks. And once I started looking properly, it's happening everywhere.'

I hadn't meant to blurt it all out. But crucially, how would Artur respond?

'You're not the first person to make such comments, Anna. Even on this base. You're right, I believe you. But what can we do?'

I fumbled a reply. 'Maybe President Putin doesn't really know what's going on. I thought, if I could contrive to see him, tell him what I'd seen, it might make him challenge his sources.'

'Or it might lead you to a slow, lingering death in the Lubyanka. You wouldn't be the first.' Artur shook his head. 'Trouble is, Anna, persuasion doesn't work in an autocracy.'

I was angry now; I wasn't here to debate. 'But we can't let one man – maybe one led astray by self-delusion – corrupt and destroy our entire country. He must listen to someone!'

Slowly, Artur shook his head. 'Bullies only understand brute force, Anna.'

I thought about his words. 'In that case, Artur, isn't there something *you* can do during the Parade? You said you'd be there.'

'That's what I keep asking myself. Hearing your description of Mariupol is my final confirmation.'

I stared at him. 'You never told me exactly what you were doing.'

'I'm in the fly-past. Putin will be centre stage below me – impossible to miss. If I peel off and crash down on top of him, no-one will be able to stop me. Don't worry, Anna. You've reached one of the few people able to take decisive action. But now you'd better leave me.'

Twenty-four hours later I watched the Parade on television. The fly-past was certain to be a major highlight.

Then came the soul-destroying words: 'The fly-past has been cancelled because of poor weather.'

Ridiculous. I looked out of the window at a clear-blue sky.

At that moment came a heavy knocking at my door.

This story won the Thames Valley Writers' Circle competition for 2022. Independent judge Iain Pattison commented:

"I loved this entry. It's a gripping, well written story with great tension, jeopardy and thrills delivered with great pace.
Protagonist Anna is beautifully sketched - a likable, gutsy woman with a strong moral code, determination and a mission to save others. This makes her immensely sympathetic.
The plot is convincing, the setting and sense of menace real, and the events unfold with increasing excitement.
The ending hits you like a hammer blow. It elicits visceral emotions. The story is tightly scripted, and the balance is perfect between optimism and a chilling sense of doom.
I haven't much more to say about this - except that I wish I'd written it."

2. CHARIOTS OF WIRE

'So here's the cottage, madam,' said estate agent John, as he led Daisy up the garden path. 'I told you it was isolated. Just needing a little Tender Loving Care.'

A gross understatement. It didn't just need repainting. A full rebuild was an alternate solution, and probably cheaper.

'It's not my object to buy it,' she replied. 'My Aunt Hilda lived here twenty years ago, before the war. I had to see it while I was on the Island.'

The agent looked deflated. The cottage had been on sale for ages. But he was a dogged man with a rehearsed spiel. 'It's early Edwardian, madam: 1907. They built them to last in those days. Especially here on the Isle of Man.'

'You mean, it's as old as the first TT Race?' Daisy had certainly done her homework.

'Indeed. Dozens of high-speed laps every spring, right round the island. Visitors flock to gawp. For locals, it's a nightmare – especially when there's a fatality.'

'Motor bikes are death-traps on hairpin bends,' agreed Daisy. 'Mind, cancelling the speed limit makes it even worse.'

The agent knew his local history. 'No-one was killed in 1907,' he protested. 'Now, would you like to see inside?'

A few moments later they were standing in the hall. Layers of dust everywhere and a musty smell, no doubt worsened by the latest heat wave.

'This hasn't been lived in recently?'

'I'm afraid not, madam. Chance for a completely fresh start,' he added brightly.

Daisy frowned. 'Let's be honest, John. Has anyone owned it after Hilda?'

'It took several years before it sold,' the agent admitted. 'You see –'

As he hesitated, Daisy broke in. 'Hilda committed suicide here. Yes, I knew that. But no-one knew why. She was still young.'

The agent reflected on his notes. These could surely be shared? He sighed.

'Trouble was, Daisy, your aunt wasn't found straight away. The one who came across her – or rather, her body – was the builder, when he came to finish plastering. Months elapsed while the death was investigated – without much success, I'm afraid. Hilda had starved to death. By the time the cottage was up for sale, a year had gone, and rumours abounded; the ghost was a celebrated feature. Which made it virtually unsellable.'

Daisy didn't speak for a few minutes as she absorbed the new information.

'I'd still like to see round, please.'

If Daisy's motive in visiting the cottage had been to find why Hilda had ended her life, she was disappointed. The cottage had been occupied occasionally over the years but there were few signs of life. No calendar in the kitchen or books by the bed. In any case, Daisy told herself, there'd been an investigation – any details had gone years ago.

'I'm afraid there aren't many clues,' John admitted. The tour was over and they'd reached the old-fashioned kitchen. But he could sense her distress and wanted to help.

'I'm so sorry, Daisy. Did Hilda die before the first TT Race – or afterwards?'

Daisy shrugged. 'No idea. Fixing the date of death was impossible in 1907. Mind, it's hardly an exact science today.'

'In those days, I'm told, new owners used to visit their intended property, to make sure the builders were completing it properly. If Hilda had been here, she'd surely have watched the first TT Race. It was the biggest event in the Island's history.'

Daisy frowned. 'Is the course far from here?'

John smiled. 'The Devil's Elbow is halfway up the hill behind us. In 1907 that was the nearest we came to a fatality.' He paused; was this too macabre? But he saw he'd caught her interest.

'Yes. The leader, two laps from the end, was Remy. Torrential rain had started, making the surface sticky. Then Remy had a puncture as he raced towards the Elbow. He skidded and lost control – went right through the crash barrier on the bend.'

'Oh, no.' Daisy buried her face in her hands. 'And was killed?'

'He was lucky he wasn't. They didn't wear helmets in those days – just facemasks.'

'But he didn't win, anyway?'

The agent took a moment to reply.

'Well, it was rather odd. He was badly shaken, ready to quit. Then one of the spectators told him he was "miles ahead". There was plenty of time. If he could mend his puncture and get back on his bike, she said, he could still be in front. And that's what happened.'

Daisy couldn't help but smile. 'Sounds like something out of a Grimm fairy tale. I bet the runner-up wasn't too happy.'

'Billy? Yeah, he was gutted. Never raced again.'

Daisy pondered for a while.

'If Hilda was visiting this cottage,' she mused, 'she might even have been a spectator on the Elbow.'

The agent nodded. 'Could have been. Each lap was miles of open countryside but most of the crowds started from a town. The Devil's Elbow was inaccessible – unless you happened to live nearby.'

Suddenly a sharp crack came from above.

Looking up, they saw the ceiling was starting to split in two. A tiny crack had appeared in the plaster. It ran from one wall towards the other, growing wider even as they watched.

'Daisy, I don't want to alarm you . . .'

But he was too late. Even as they turned towards the doorway the plaster started falling around them. One large piece caught Daisy on the shoulder. She cried out, stumbled and fell. Then more pieces crashed down, many landing on top of her. With huge clouds of the grey dust that had accumulated over decades. It looked. . . well, like a war zone.

For a minute Daisy couldn't see the doorway; the agent could scarcely see her. The noise was terrifying. It seemed to go on and on.

Probably, the whole cataclysmic episode took less than five minutes. But the impact on the two occupants was severe.

'Daisy. . . Daisy!! Are you alright?'

There was a pause; then the agent heard a moan from the pile of rubble on the floor. Thank goodness; at least she was still alive.

'I think so,' said a croaky voice. 'Just battered and bruised.'

But time was not on their side. Being patient was not an option. 'Daisy, we've got to get out. The rest might come down any minute.'

He picked his way through the fallen plaster towards her. 'Here, give us your arm. You can't stay down there.'

Neither could say, afterwards, how they'd even made it. But ten minutes later they had dragged themselves outside and collapsed on the overgrown lawn. Neither was bleeding; but the choking dust left them dry and parched, unable to speak. For Daisy, who had suffered the most, the shock induced near-hysterical laughter.

Twenty minutes went by before they had collected themselves sufficiently to take stock.

Daisy felt her face. There was something not there.

'I've got to go back in,' she gasped. 'I'm missing my glasses. They must be somewhere in the kitchen.'

'You can't, Daisy. It's not safe.'

But the dusty, crusty Daisy was long past caring. Without her glasses she was half blind. She pulled herself up and hobbled inside. Her glasses were still on the floor, among the debris. Badly in need of a clean but, miraculously, not broken.

She was returning when she noticed something else. A large brown envelope had come down with the plaster. It was marked with a strange, three-legged symbol, drawn inside a large circle.

'Whatever's this, John?'

The agent took it, turned it over and eyed the hand-drawn symbol. 'I know that. It's the first Tourist Trophy Race logo. It must have been up in the ceiling since 1907. You'd best open it.'

He watched silently as Daisy unsealed the envelope.

The first item was a faded copy of the Manx Times for June 1907. It described the first TT Race in detail, including the turning point on the Devil's Elbow.

The spectator wasn't named, but the word had been circled. And the word "me!" was pencilled alongside.

There was also a hand-written letter.

To my eventual reader.

I'll be gone before this is found. But I have nothing left to live for. My beloved Billy found out what I'd done on the Elbow and was incandescent. I tried so hard to explain, but it was no use.

"It was raining," I told him. "I couldn't see behind the face mask - thought it was you. You'd boasted to me you'd be leading from the start."

Billy growled. "I've been robbed of victory. I'll never race again."

Then he walked out, slammed the door and locked me in. Mounted his chariot and powered away. It was clear he never wanted to see me again.

There's no food in the cottage now. I'm desperately hungry. For day after day I've hoped someone would visit. The builder, for instance. He's got to come back: the kitchen ceiling still needs plastering.

But no one has come. I don't think they ever will.

Just got to hide this letter. I'm very weak now. When Billy does hear I've gone, I hope he will feel guilty.

I loved you to the end, Billy. Pity the end has come so soon.

Hilda

3 HENDERSONS' RELISH

When first married, Sally and Miles Henderson were best-known among friends for their bickering.

That was mainly because, in so many ways, they were opposites. Miles was a cautious man with the mind of a chess player: always thinking several moves ahead. It was alleged (with some truth) that his main passion was hitting closing deadlines.

Whereas his shapely wife didn't plan at all: she was outgoing and generous, empathetic and willing to take all sorts of risks.

But they gradually learned to work together. They were in the decorating business.

Here, at least, their differences proved complementary. Miles would compute quotes for jobs in fine detail, including everything that might go wrong. He was rarely undercut. Once they'd got a job, Sally would take the lead on design. And when work was needed, say, to repaint a ceiling, she was always the one balanced on top, while her husband steadied the ladder and removed the sticky paint droplets down below.

Together they were "completer-finishers"; and their reputation spread. The light-grey Henderson van, carrying its dark-purple S&M symbol, was often seen around the district.

The only point where professional disagreements could arise was in quoting for new jobs. Miles always feared not getting the business: was his price sufficiently low? But Sally, when she had the chance, would bid high. Given a newly-decorated property with a need for new soft furnishing, she could devise all sorts of ways of adding to its value – and also charging for the privilege.

Local commendation had given them a new customer, Howard. He owned a three-storey house in Sheffield's Harcourt Road, backing onto park and lake. When they were invited to assess it, Miles couldn't see there was much interior redecorating needed at all. Although the magnolia, in room after room, was perhaps overdone.

But Sally perceived a man of wealth, who was bound to benefit from a more striking home. It was she who, despite her husband's frowns, pushed successfully for a free hand on the decor and an open-ended budget.

'I'm in Paris this month,' Howard told them. 'Back on June 30th. Hopefully with a long-term companion. Can it be done by then?'

To the Hendersons, a whole month to work in an empty house was a luxury and a price was agreed. The work began next day.

Both Hendersons threw themselves into their new commission. Miles was acutely aware that Sally had been responsible for the price they'd be able to charge. He allowed her to select each room's colours, which had to alternate from room to room. As she wandered round with her colour charts, he began the preparation. That always seemed to make up an unfairly large chunk of the total decorating time.

No-one knocked at the door and the telephone did not ring. Miles relished the freedom to work at his own pace. But after a few days silence, Sally wondered what that said about Howard's friends and neighbours. Weren't any of them missing him? He hadn't seemed lonely on their only meeting, but was he shy? And who was this "companion" he hoped to return with? They hadn't dared to ask; but did he intend to return with a partner – or a bride? Might she (assuming it was a she) not have a strong colour sense of her own?

Howard would surely appreciate a few romantic refinements in the place, once the main decoration was finished. Sally mused over alternative options as the decorating progressed; and used her occasional afternoons off to buy in relevant materials.

It was late on June 29th when Miles declared their work was complete: the house was fully decorated. He would work from home next day, calculating and assembling the bill.

Meanwhile, Sally grabbed her chance to enhance the core decorations and enliven Howard's return. She wanted to make sure the overall concept was accepted wholeheartedly.

Firstly she had her hair refashioned. Off came her long brown hair. Instead she acquired a pixie bob with highlights. As she'd hoped, it made her look a lot younger.

She'd passed a flower shop. On her return she bought bunches with matching colours for every room. Back in Harcourt Road she spent some time freshening the house up.

She also bought scented candles and candleholders for the master bedroom.

Then she gave the master bed a new duvet cover. And replaced the dour curtains (which looked like they'd been there for decades) with smart new ones: attractive spring-flower patterns, to go with the new cover.

Finally, Sally had a shower and changed out of her regular jump suit into the best dress the local charity shop could offer. And lit most of the candles. She was desperate to give the best impression.

At half past three a vehicle drew up outside. Glancing out she saw Howard alighting from a taxi.

But something must have gone badly wrong. He was on his own.

Sally recalled her object: she was here to welcome Howard to his "new" home, to make sure he appreciated the new décor. A large amount of money was due, which rested on a good reception. Quickly she raced downstairs. She was just in time to open the front door.

'Welcome home, Howard.' Her voice had grown husky from four weeks hard labour. Would he recognise her?

'Decorating finished yesterday,' she continued. 'I'm here to show you round.'

He looked bemused. Maybe he'd had a long journey? Or a bust-up with his companion on the way?

But once inside the hall he was positively gobsmacked.

'Wow. This is fabulous.'

They traversed room after room. Sally let Howard set the pace. In each area he made a warm response, relishing the striking colour mixes.

Finally she led him upstairs and into the master bedroom.

It wasn't exactly as she'd planned it: he didn't have a companion to be swept off her feet. Was the romantic regime going to be wasted?

Or perhaps she had overdone it. For Howard eased off his jacket and shoes and lay on the bed, focusing on her intently. To her horror, she realised he was hoping for more.

'The end of the tour,' she announced firmly. 'I hope you're satisfied with everything that we've done?'

But Howard was still on the tour bus.

She could only play for time. Sally racked her brains.

'You know, I don't have to be as dressed up quite as formally as this,' she murmured.

This time she could see she'd hit the button. Howard was almost beside himself in anticipation. There was no going back now.

It was ten to four. Slowly, ever so slowly – there was every reason not to hurry – Sally reached behind her back. The waistline bow needed unfastening. That could take some time.

There was a moment of panic when it stuck fast; then the ribbon was released.

But Howard was after more than mild titillation. He said nothing but continued to stare at her intently. She was trapped; couldn't see any way off the pathway she'd started.

Once more she reached behind her back until she felt the zip. Seizing it, she pulled down and felt her dress loosening.

This was the moment.

She reached up and drew the garment from her shoulders, dropped it slowly onto the floor.

And stood before him, dressed only in the flimsiest of lacy underwear.

Howard's eyes almost popped out of his head. He looked her slowly up and down, then down and up.

It did nothing at all for her, but there was no doubt she was pleasing her client.

But now they had reached the point where, for her own sanity, their paths had to diverge.

At that second came a ding from the doorbell.

Sally peered out of the window. The Henderson van was parked outside.

'It's Miles,' she gasped.

The name seemed to bring Howard out of his fantasy. The respectable houseowner was suddenly restored.

'There's a fire escape ladder at the back,' he declared, as he led her to a window at the rear and opened it.

Sally had no option but to climb out onto the ladder, a rusty one that they'd never thought to repaint. She was hardly dressed for an outdoor ride. And it was a long way down.

There was a bang above her and Howard closed the window. He disappeared, presumably to deal with Miles. She was on her own. She just had to descend fifty steps to ground level, rung by rusty rung.

Sally was a feisty woman: if she didn't look down it might be manageable. Until to her dismay, her lower foot couldn't feel anything at all. The next rung was no longer there – or if it was, it was well out of reach. And gritting her teeth, holding on tightly and glancing down, she saw that the whole lowest stretch of the ladder was missing.

The hard choice was to remain dangling outdoors in her flimsy underwear; or drop twenty feet to the garden below.

'I liked the showgirl, Miles,' said Howard. 'More glamorous than your wife, anyway.'

Miles wasn't sure how to take that. 'I hope I didn't disrupt anything. We'd agreed I'd come at four. Have we done it OK?'

Howard glanced around once more at the new décor and smiled. 'Even better than I'd hoped.'

He opened the bill, glanced at the bottom line, and nodded. 'Highly reasonable.'

It was almost midnight when Sally reached home. After half an hour's dithering, by now extremely cold, she'd finally let go; and to her horror had landed inside a butt of cold water. It took a while to climb out.

Shocked, soaked, shivering and semi-naked, she daren't even head for home across the park until it was too dark even to be seen.

'Been for a swim?' asked Miles, when she finally got home. He was in an unexpectedly cheerful mood.

'It was a very tiny pool. But tell me, did Howard pay?'

Miles gave her a broad grin. 'In full. With a tip, he said, for the showgirl.'

Sally wasn't sure how to take that; or what it might mean to Miles. Best to move on.

'You cut it mighty fine,' she observed.

'I was here at four,' he protested. 'Exactly as I promised. I may be dull – but I'm always on time.'

4   SECOND SIGHT

Justice Ellwood stared round the Inquiry Room, feeling close to despair. One wall held huge, blown-up photographs of the fifteen people who'd been killed in the recent concert hall explosion, several not yet identified. Another, more sparsely spread, held the key evidence so far gathered. The collection was hardly overwhelming.

He turned back to his lead investigator.

'So, despite all your digging, Jenkins, both physical and interpersonal, Security has no idea who was behind all this? We don't even know if the instigator was one of those killed, or is still roaming the streets?'

'Not yet, sir.'

'But you do have a full account of the recent life of Cosmic Cara?'

Jenkins nodded.

'Tell me, again, why you know so little about the one; and so much about the other.'

Jenkins gritted his teeth. Ellwood had already dragged him through this mismatch the day before.

'On the day before the concert,' he began, 'Cara appeared on Breakfast TV. She spoke of a forthcoming disaster here in Chichester. Said it would kill dozens and injure many others. There was limited reaction on the day. But there was far more, a day later, after the explosion.'

'Ah. You mean, Jenkins, National Security has come to believe in second sight? You wanted Cara to tell you how?'

'It's not that, sir,' the investigator protested.

'You, presumably, don't believe it was pure coincidence – not just luck on her part?'

Jenkins sighed. 'We've gone through Cara's earlier predictions, sir. Despite her psychic reputation, they are less clear-cut and endlessly repeated. This one, though, seemed more authoritative. And timely.'

'I take it that she has been interviewed?'

'Extensively. She was happy to talk, after a period of solitude. Of course, she's not under arrest. We've no evidence to charge her. Foreknowledge is not itself a crime.'

Ellwood gave a heartfelt sigh and then pressed on. 'And what had she to say about this prediction? How long had she held it, for example?'

'Less than a week, sir. It came on a train journey near Stonehenge.'

Ellwood's face was a study in horror: this inquiry was getting out of control. But he could see no choice but to persevere.

'D'you know which train?'

'The 10:30 from Salisbury: it's a local service to Trowbridge. Southern Rail have been very helpful. They've given us a CCTV image of every passenger on board. Though in fact, on the morning in question, there weren't that many.'

It felt to Ellwood like he was trying to suck blood out of a stone. 'And were any of them known to Security?'

'There was no-one in our "most-suspect" category, sir. But we've been going through them again. There was one passenger matched up later, from our "fringe" list. We identified him; turned out, from reference to British Airways, that he'd just returned from Libya.'

For Ellwood, at last, some new information. He beamed. 'And you've interviewed him?'

This time Jenkins was laconic. 'We haven't been able to find him. Which, I guess, is suspicious in itself.'

'But you'll have shown his picture to Cara? Did she know him? Does she admit to meeting him on that train?'

This time Jenkins hesitated. He was aware he didn't have the answer the Justice was hoping for.

'She says she's not sure, sir; she's met a lot of people since then. And the camera at Salisbury station, where the picture was taken, is wide-angled, so our image of each passenger is tiny. Enlargement any only makes them fuzzier.'

There was a baffled silence.

This was hard work, thought Justice Ellwood; he had to appear positive. Jenkins and the others were doing their best. The trouble was, their best was nowhere near enough.

'Let's suppose, Jenkins,' said the Justice, 'that this was a key encounter – how Cosmic Cara got her inside information. Is there any way to find the names of other passengers on that train? I don't mean the security suspect; I mean ordinary citizens. Ones you could interview. Someone must have seen something.'

'I left one of my team working on that, sir. But it may take us a couple of days.'

Two days later the Inquiry resumed.

'Right, Jenkins,' said Justice Ellwood. 'What have you got?'

For once the lead investigator was looking cheerful. 'I think we might have been lucky, sir.'

'Go on.'

'My team kept telling me that, as time passed, it was harder to get any passengers to come forward. All the CCTV pictures we had were minute. But then my analyst spotted that one passenger on the train was wearing a dog collar: they were a vicar.

27

That narrowed the field hugely.'

'What happened next?'

'We contacted the local police, and hence the Bishop of Salisbury. Explained the urgency of the inquiry and sent him our pictures. A Salisbury vicar called us a couple of hours later. Said he'd been on the 10:30 morning train to Trowbridge; and asked how he could help.'

'And then?'

'I interviewed him over the phone. He told me he'd been sitting across the aisle, almost opposite Cosmic Cara. He was worried that she'd start bothering him. Apparently, sir, she's notorious for taking a particular dislike to clergymen – regards them as a competing form of wisdom. But before she could get to him, a North African gentleman came down the aisle and grabbed the seat opposite her. The vicar had a ring-side seat for the whole encounter.'

'But is a phone interview proper evidence?' mused the Justice.

'I told him I was recording it. Afterwards I got my secretary to type it up and send it through for him to sign. It's authentic enough.'

'Good. Go on then.'

'The African seemed to recognise Cosmic Cara. She always dresses in bright colours and a silver-lined, multi-layered gown. She's often on TV, so that's not a surprise. He seemed to be pleading for help.'

'Could the vicar overhear what was being said?'

'Well, the two had a long conversation. Unfortunately with hushed voices, so my vicar couldn't tell me what they were talking about. But it led on to an exchange.'

By this time the Justice was practically on the edge of his seat. 'Don't keep us in suspense, Jenkins.'

'Right, sir. I don't think Cosmic Cara ever travels light. On this occasion she had a massive holdall, containing odds and ends that perhaps might be useful to the folk she talked to. She opened it up, poked around, then produced an old army knapsack. Which she handed over to the African.'

Ellwood blinked. 'Was that what he was after?'

'He seemed happy enough, anyway. My clerical witness noticed that he didn't seem to have any luggage of his own – except whatever was in his various coat pockets. But the gift made him want to respond to Cara in some way. He produced a sheet of paper and wrote down a message, very carefully.'

At last he was being presented with some sharp investigation. 'Well done, Jenkins,' said the Justice. 'You've really got something to confront Cosmic Cara with now.'

Jenkins smiled again. 'We've already done that, sir. Another low-key interview.'

'Good. So what's her latest story?'

'Cara accepted the whole account I put to her. Didn't argue with any of it. She said the man asked her if she had some sort of bag. Once he'd been given the rucksack, he exchanged it for a prediction. Which was almost exactly the words she spoke in her television "prophecy".'

'You've arrested her, I hope?'

'Not yet, sir. You see, she went on to say that the whole incident left her extremely worried. So when she got to Trowbridge, her first action, once off the train, was to find a police officer and tell him what had happened. She also handed over the forecast.'

'And this was . . .?'

'Five days before the bomb went off.'

There was a long, uncomfortable silence in the Inquiry Room.

But it couldn't last.

'Have you . . . have you taken this line of inquiry any further, Jenkins?'

Jenkins looked embarrassed now. 'I have, sir. I rang Trowbridge Police Station late yesterday afternoon. Talked to their senior officer. He knew nothing about it. But I'm awaiting a call back, once he does. I'm horribly afraid we are going to uncover a massive "own goal" in the security services.'

Justice Ellwood did not speak. He thanked his lucky stars that this part of the Inquiry was taking place behind closed doors. There was plenty here for the media to make trouble with – if they ever got hold of the full story.

Suddenly he had an idea. 'Jenkins, can you find me that list of possessions which they found after the explosion, please.'

There followed a few untidy moments while Jenkins' colleagues waded through large folders, gathering the information requested. He pulled it together and presented it all to the Justice.

'I'm afraid this is all we've got, sir. It's not much. It was a truly massive explosion, destroyed almost everything.'

There was silence in the Inquiry Room as the Justice thumbed slowly through the extracts.

Then it was his turn to smile.

'Look here: it says the "remains of a metal buckle". Couldn't that be from an old army knapsack? And we are told below that it was "next to parts of an unidentified body".

'Can we ask Cara if the buckle's from her rucksack? If it is, I'd say it's almost certain that this unknown body, whom we've had down as a bomb victim, was in fact the perpetrator. We can even say how he carried the bomb.'

Much later, behind the scenes, Justice Ellwood met Cosmic

Cara and attempted to pay her a tribute.

'It's only thanks to your evidence, Cara, that we were able to identify the bomber.'

But Cara didn't want praise. 'Please don't say too much, sir. The "prophecy" has done my professional reputation no harm at all. I don't want all my secrets in the public domain.'

5   HENDERSONS' RETURN

Once we'd settled down, Miles Henderson and I were a happily married couple. There was always plenty of intimacy. But one day my husband discovered that I was ticklish.

Not just a tiny bit; I was an excessive giggler. Once, during a bouncy session, I shouted so loudly that the neighbours came knocking on our front door to check I was alright.

After that we always went upstairs. The challenge was to see for how long he could tickle me before I begged for mercy. Was he too rough? Not really. The games were only played on my invitation and when I was in the mood. I was the one in charge; and could call a halt at any time.

I told him he was lucky to be married to a feisty woman. After all, it didn't affect our business. We were decorators.

Miles provided the planning; I contributed the flair. I had an instinct for colour-blending and soft furnishing. We'd take on any job, inside or out; and were locally famous for doing it well.

One March we received an invitation from Howard. He was an old customer; he'd hired us last year to redecorate his entire house. 'Please,' it read, 'come to my Spring Exchange.'

'Wow,' I said. 'That's a surprise. We're hardly friends.' As you may remember, I'd had a perilously close encounter with Howard during the final decorating handover.

'But it's great,' enthused Miles. 'Howard's well-off; he'll have wealthy friends. When we're there his new décor will speak on our behalf. Might even lead to more business.'

I wasn't enthusiastic. I'd seen too much of Howard already (and, in a different way, him of me). 'It sounds too posh, Miles. Why can't he just say "Party"?'

'Sally, that's not a word the upper class use anymore. It has . . . connotations.'

I thought for a moment. 'But is it a dinner, or a dance, or what? What am I supposed to wear?' Even to my ears my excuse sounded feeble.

As we pondered, I thought of a bigger obstacle. 'Miles, I'm afraid Howard will think of "Sally" as a dowdy woman, mostly used to wielding the paintbrush.'

'Then he's in for a pleasant surprise, darling. Get yourself a new outfit. If we win some new business it'll be worth it.'

'But. . .'

My voice tailed away. I'd never recounted the finer details of my last visit to Howard's; and my diplomatic husband had chosen not to ask. I'd need a dress that didn't look anything like the one I'd worn before. I mustn't look like a showgirl.

As the date approached, I visited big shops and returned with a fresh hairstyle and a new dress, plus accessories and shoes. This was the upside of Howard's invitation – Miles virtually never encouraged me to buy a new outfit. I didn't dare show him the bill.

We walked round to Howard's. 'It's quiet,' I observed. 'Maybe we've got the wrong day? If so, it might be sticky.'

'Don't worry, Sally. We're probably the first ones here. Someone has to be.'

Miles rang the doorbell and Howard appeared, wearing a shiny jacket and a smart bow tie. My heart sank: it was the right evening. He recognised my husband at once.

'Welcome, Miles. So glad you could come.'

He turned towards me, not recognising me at all. But for some reason the socially innocuous Miles saw no need to introduce me.

I felt let down. Disinclined to rescue my partner. Then I had a naughty thought: could I prolong the confusion?

'I'm Salome,' I claimed, 'friend of Miles. Sally couldn't come. Howard, have we met? Hey, are we the first?'

Miles gave me a puzzled look but said nothing.

Our host led us into the elegantly painted lounge, inspecting me carefully. Maybe, distantly, he half recognised me. But only as a showgirl. I'd not told him my name on that hard-to-forget occasion.

I smiled inwardly: this might become an interesting evening.

Howard offered us generous helpings of wine and nibbles and took a glass for himself. 'The fact you're first gives us a chance to introduce ourselves. Why don't I begin?'

He drank some wine before launching. 'My work is supporting independent filmmaking across Europe. That's why I was in Paris last summer. I'm always on the lookout for fresh ideas.'

He turned to Miles. 'I loved your technical work in this house, especially Sally's kaleidoscope of colours. They blend beautifully. Would the pair of you ever consider an occasional role in filmmaking?'

Miles pretended to ponder. Was this why they'd been invited? I could read his mind. The chance of a life away from mixing paint and shinning up ladders, then coming home to a sad account.

But that wasn't going to work: it was my flair that Howard was after.

Miles tried to make amends.

'I'm so sorry Sally couldn't be with us tonight. . . she had an unexpected migraine.'

Howard nodded. 'Right. You know, I was wondering why you'd brought Salome.'

I wanted to help, could see more explanation was needed. 'Miles and I've known one another for years. I was glad to step in.'

'Are you connected with the decorating business?'

'I sometimes dream up symbols and other marketing objects.'

Now the penny dropped. Howard eyed me sharply. 'You know, Salome, I reckon you've been here before. You're the lovely lady who showed me round, after I got back from Paris.'

So he hadn't forgotten the unscripted striptease. 'Yes. That was me.' Best to change the subject, I thought, before Miles gleaned any more. 'What sort of films d'you make, Howard?'

Now it was his turn to be coy. 'Ah, that's a commercial secret, my dear.' He paused, took an even bigger swig of his wine and gave a mischievous smile. 'Mind, I could say more if I was talking to prospective colleagues.'

This was all moving too fast. Miles intervened. 'D'you mean you'd give us an informal interview, Howard?'

'I was hoping for an exploratory chat with you and Sally. Trouble is, I'm not sure how Salome can help us.'

Miles took another swig of his wine. It seemed to embolden him: he couldn't miss an opportunity like this. It was not often that fame beckoned. Suddenly an idea came that might satisfy Howard's curiosity.

'Well. I happen to know that Salome is ticklish.'

I couldn't help it, I started to cough. Then I saw him staring at me and turned it into a half-hearted laugh. Whatever was he saying? Tickling was private. I had to think quickly.

'I'm afraid that I always giggle too loudly, Howard. We couldn't do anything like that here. We'd disturb your neighbours.'

It was a good rebuttal. One I was proud of. But as I'd seen before, Howard, once alerted, wasn't easily thwarted.

'There's one room here, Miles, that you never painted: the cellar. It's my den; locked and completely soundproof. How about we all take a look?'

Howard unlocked the hall doorway and led us downstairs: a soundproofed ceiling, a desk, various chairs and some wall bars. 'I like to keep fit,' he explained.

But he hadn't brought us down simply to show off his den. 'How does it usually happen, Miles?' He obviously had ideas of his own.

I could guess where the conversation was heading. I'd seen Miles' bright-eyed response to the talk of working in films. It would be worth so much to him, maybe even help our bank balance. After all, he was my husband. I didn't want to completely obstruct him.

As I've said before, I'm a feisty woman, willing to take a few risks. No doubt Howard recalled what had happened last time; I could live with the same thing happening again. From where we'd reached it might be best to be proactive.

'If you want to see Miles tickle me, Howard, I'd better take my dress off. It's brand new, I don't want to risk it getting crumpled. But nothing more: that's as far as I'm going.'

Miles looked guilty. He knew mentioning tickling had been a bad mistake. He'd suffer reprisals from me later. But the remote prospect of a career in films had beckoned. He too could see no way back.

36

'There are various games we play, Howard,' he said. 'Usually I tickle Salome till she surrenders.'

Howard wanted at least some of the action. 'Or I could make up a message and whisper it to Salome. See how long it takes you to tickle it out of her. If it's more than five minutes then I'm the winner.'

Whoever the winner was, it wasn't going to be me. I could only trust myself to Miles' protection.

I slipped my dress off. The men removed their jackets and ties and the game began.

They played "tickle my secret" till I pleaded exhaustion. 'Guys, I can't do this anymore.'

But Howard had another idea. 'You know, there is a more famous Salome. She danced so well before Herod that he offered her a prize. That's how John the Baptist lost his head.'

Miles observed wryly, 'I can see why you're into films, Howard.'

I nodded, though without enthusiasm. But Howard was thirsting for a spectacle.

I gritted my teeth. 'I could give it a try, I suppose. Though please let me start with my dress on. And I insist on suitable music. I'm sure Salome didn't dance in total silence.'

But that roadblock didn't work either. Howard had sound-making equipment down here. I got fully dressed again while seductive music was selected. Miles was trying hard to slow the process.

Finally the delays were over. Howard and Miles were ready for my performance.

Then the doorbell rang.

Howard gave a disappointed sigh. 'Ah, that must be my other guests. Salome, my dear, you look ravishing. Would you mind going to let them in? Miles and I will have to wash and tidy ourselves up.'

As I returned upstairs, I reminded myself: I was the architect of my downfall. As I reached the hall I saw the cellar key, was sorely tempted to lock the two men in. Somehow, I managed to resist.

Ten minutes later a more conventional party was beginning in the lounge. Our suave, bow-tied host was once more serving drinks as though nothing had happened at all.

Much later, back home, we asked ourselves some searching questions. The film-making discussion had got no further.

'Would any of that have happened, Miles, if I'd not claimed to be someone else?'

'Possibly not,' he replied. 'But it wasn't you. It was my fault for mentioning tickling.'

We mused for a while on the events of the evening.

'Goodness knows where Howard might have wanted me to go as Salome.'

I sighed with relief. 'Good job the other guests turned up when they did.'

Miles smiled. 'I knew they'd be there by nine. I'd seen the time on their invitations.'

'What??'

He nodded. 'Yes. Didn't I tell you? I got chatting to one of 'em in the pub last week. We argued over when the event started, and he was carrying his invitation. He knew Howard's "exchanges". So he could give me a foretaste of what to expect. But my dear, you played along beautifully.'

I wasn't sure how to respond.

'I admit I sometimes like a good tickle, Miles. But in future, please, only in private. No more public performances – ever.'

6   SENIOR GOLF

The request was a shock to the Club Secretary at the Dog. It came from the American Embassy; and asserted that two very senior golfers wanted to play a game at the club without anyone else present – apart for a couple of local caddies. Laurie and Greg happened to be there for their weekly round and were "volunteered" for the role.

'Mind, we've never caddied before,' murmured Laurie.

'Ideal,' said the Secretary. 'It's all in the act, anyway. The main thing is you know the course, and especially the surrounding bushes. I doubt these guys will be that fussy about rules and etiquette.'

He issued a notice closing the course for Thursday in two weeks' time; and hired a two-seater buggy from a prestigious club nearby. The Dog hadn't any buggies of their own. He also managed to acquire professional outfits for the two caddies.

Someone from the Embassy even came round to check everything beforehand.

On the Thursday Laurie and Greg were there early and donned their uniforms. A huge car bumped down the track and a large, orange-faced man got out, fair hair splaying in all directions. He looked faintly familiar as he headed towards the clubroom.

'I can see why they ordered a buggy,' muttered Greg. 'Hope his opponent's a bit thinner.'

The Secretary rushed out to greet him, then brought him

over to meet the caddies. 'Donald, Greg will be your caddy today. He knows the course and its surroundings like the back of his hand.'

'Great to meet you, Greg. Good job you weren't needed this week for the Ryder Cup.' He guided his caddie outside for a private briefing.

'See, I don't hold with all these rules. It's a simple game and I play in a simple way. Here's a couple of dozen golf balls, all with the same crest and number: they're interchangeable. I'm not here to poke around in the bushes, Greg. I'm here to win. Anything you can do to make sure that happens is fine with me. I'll make sure you benefit when I do.'

As they continued talking round the side of the hut, his opponent arrived: tall and bronzed, with a cheery smile. Once more the Secretary greeted him. 'Bill, this is your caddie: Laurie. He's local but he knows the course inside out – and all the short-cuts.'

Bill smiled: sounded like his sort of golfer. 'Laurie, I'm happy to take any advice on short cuts and strategies. It'd be good to win, but I'm here mainly to build links with my opponent. We know each other far too well as politicians, it'd be good to relate as golfers.'

The two seniors managed to squeeze into the buggy; Donald seized the wheel and they set off for the first hole. Greg and Laurie walked steadily behind them, each struggling with a massive bag of clubs.

At the first tee the golfers disembarked and approached their caddies for driver, ball and tee. Their drivers were huge. They each performed various opening exercises.

'You know, Bill,' said Donald, 'it seems odd to be playing without a huge crowd of hangers-on.'

'That's what we agreed, Donald. I reckon you and I have overdosed on publicity.'

Greg tossed a coin and Bill chose correctly. 'Right, Donald, why don't you go first.'

His opponent teed up and settled himself, with a few practice swings. Then he swung in earnest. There was a fierce "thwack". His ball soared high into the air, heading for the flag. Then it caught the breeze, swung to the left and landed in the gorse bushes bordering the fairway.

A few minutes later Bill had performed a similar manoeuvre. His shot had achieved a similar length but was sliced, landing in the bushes on the opposite side.

The two golfers clambered into their buggy, smiling cheerfully, and headed up the fairway. The caddies hastened to catch them up.

'We'll do our best to find them,' said Greg, once they'd reached the approximate location. He consoled himself that he could replace Donald's ball, assuming the first one was lost.

Laurie had been similarly armed with replacement balls. It was only a few minutes before the golfers could take their second shots from either side of the fairway.

The green was less than a hundred yards away. Donald, confusing his ball with Planet Earth, mishit and was just short; but Bill overhit into the bushes beyond. As his opponent headed over the green in pursuit, Donald walked up to his ball and gave it a nifty kick onto the green. 'Like I said, Greg, I'm gonna win, one way or another.'

Laurie had seen what happened but realised it wasn't his place to protest. The first hole had gone to Donald.

It would be too painful to followers of golf – and too tedious to everyone else – to describe the round that followed in much detail.

The level of cheating rose steadily. Bill was no more enamoured of the rules than Donald. Both regarded replacing a ball onto the fairway and kicking it closer to the hole as necessary parts of positioning their ball for the next shot. Especially if there happened to be a bunker on the desired line of flight, between its current position and the flag.

Once a ball actually landed in a bunker – as happened quite often – the distinction between practise swings and intended shots was lost entirely.

On strict golfing rules, a lost ball should incur a two-stroke penalty. But since each player had come armed with many identical replacements, the balls were never officially lost at all.

The caddies were drawn into a meta game behind the apparent game of golf. Donald and Bill were relying on the pair to record the score. But they didn't check their work. As the two friends worked together, there was plenty of scope for accepting near misses beside the flag and also for ignoring failed shots in a bunker. Also for registering a standard two shots to get out of a bunker, however many were actually taken.

The recorded scores remained fairly level. The two golfers agreed early on that they would track only which golfer won each hole and not worry about exactly how many shots each player had taken. In many cases the level of cheating was such that holes were shared.

As the round continued and the later score became tied, the mood between the senior golfers lightened. Once, many years ago, they had been friends. Now, as their buggy started on a long traverse to a more distant tee, they started to recall some of the difficult incidents that had divided them; and to reconstruct them in a better light.

'I saw a lot of your Hillary in my presidential debates, Bill. I'd never say so in public, but she's quite a girl.'

'She was as scared as hell, Donald. The candidates are in the spotlight, they can hardly see the audience at all – it's like walking down a darkened lane with your worst enemy. D'you remember that time when you crept up behind her as she was outlining her defence priorities? It looked to many of us like you were intending to assault her.'

Donald nodded. 'I was certainly hoping to frighten her. She didn't flinch, though. She's a gutsy woman, you know. You need to hang onto her.'

There was a pause as the buggy negotiated a rutted corner. Then Bill recalled an earlier incident. 'I nearly did lose her once, of course. Over that intern, Monica. Mind, she was a fun woman. Understood how to make a man content.' He smiled. 'I'd say those were some of my happiest days in the White House.'

Donald thought about the relationship. Like everyone else he'd followed the scandal on television. 'How did you manage to find any privacy? When I was living in the White House, security staff were roaming everywhere.'

Bill gave a conspiratorial grin. 'Ah. There was a back corridor between the West Wing and the Oval Office, a short cut with no CCTV cameras at all. I used to muddle my diary so everyone thought I was somewhere else. Then Monica and I had our playtime.' He stopped speaking, chuckling as he recalled the sequence of encounters.

'Hey, Bill, I never found that corridor. Maybe they blocked it in after you left?'

'I doubt it. The entrance was hidden behind the military coat stand. Have a look the next time you're living there.'

Donald shook his head. 'You know, Bill, I'm not sure

there's going to be a "next time". These days there seem to be even more rules in politics than there are in golf, most of 'em equally tiresome and tiring. It's rather good being out of it. Playing golf like this, without any audience at all, seems to bring out the best in me. Should we do this again?'

Later, when the game was over and the two seniors had made an amicable departure after generously tipping their caddies, Laurie and Greg considered having a game of their own.

'No need to be pedantic about the rules,' observed Greg. 'Take our lead from our seniors.'

'But what should we make of it? Have you and I really caddied for two of the once-most-popular politicians in the Western world? Or were they just a pair of well-attired actors?'

It wasn't an easy question. Then Greg felt inside his caddie jacket for a coin to decide who would tee off first and felt something else as well. 'Hey, what's this?'

He produced a gadget; it was a micro-recorder. Laurie found he had one too and frowned. 'So it wasn't just casual actors. Someone took the whole thing very seriously indeed.'

'Hey, d'you reckon there's anything similar on the buggy?' The vehicle had been left parked beside the hut. They hadn't planned to use it, but it wouldn't be collected till next day.

Laurie strode over and inspected the folding roof. Then came a shout of triumph. 'Here it is.' He showed Greg another micro-recorder.

'That's the crucial one, Laurie. What were Donald and Bill discussing as they went round? Someone was making sure it wasn't as private as they had imagined.'

They gave it a few moments thought.

'But should we help them, Greg? Wouldn't it be much better to let the seniors keep their privacy? I'd say they really enjoyed themselves. Let them keep whatever they told one another as a real secret.'

Greg mused. 'Let's think this through. I'd say the only people tracking them and capable of planting recorders like this are the CIA. If we take the recorders with us, they'll be after us for ever. The safest thing to do, I'd say, is to drop them all in the nearest duckpond.'

Which, after a few minutes' consideration, was what they did.

The pax between Donald and Bill never reached the public domain. It remains to be seen how much that will matter in the days ahead.

Even the finest golf courses are often empty in November

7 SILVER LINING

George Goode pushed her bicycle slowly along the pavement towards the local repair shop. Its front wheel was badly buckled. It had been that sort of a week – though now it was a bright autumn Saturday morning.

Outside the shop, a tall, rugged man was busy locking a smart racing bike into one of the display stands. He looked up as she approached.

'I guess the new design didn't quite work?' he observed, glancing at her mechanical nightmare.

'Bloody pothole,' she replied. 'I wouldn't have gone over it, but I was trapped into the kerb by a great big trailer lorry. And that was Westminster – supposedly the richest Council in the country.'

The man could see that some reassurance was necessary. 'I'd say you're doing well, trying to cycle in central London at all.'

George shrugged. 'I can't afford a car. And the trains don't go close to where I work.'

She turned and was about to go into the shop when something about him struck her. 'Hey. Aren't you one of the lads in Bramston Road?'

He grinned. 'Fame at last. Well spotted. Yes, I'm a Bramston Pickle. One of five, actually. We haven't been there too long.' He paused. 'So you must be from around these parts too?'

George smiled. 'Good deduction. I'm from just around the corner: Furness Road. With two other women. I've just graduated: joined their house three months ago. We haven't yet started calling ourselves the Furness Furies.'

There was a short pause. She was enjoying the encounter and in no particular hurry.

'Right,' she said. 'I suppose I'd better go in, negotiate a repair for my broken wheel.'

'I'm into bikes,' he asserted. 'Can I take a quick look?'

George wasn't going to dissent from free advice. He crouched down beside the bike and gave the wheel a wrench.

'Hm. At least two spokes are broken. In fact, the whole wheel is pretty twisted. Did you try to ride it further, after you'd hit the pothole?'

'A hundred yards or so,' she admitted. 'Then it wouldn't go at all. I had to push the wreckage all the way to the office. Then explain why I was late. I'd missed half the week's briefing, you see. That's a major crime where I work.'

There was a short pause. The man nodded towards the shop. 'They'll sell you replacement spokes alright. Make sure you get the right size. Trouble is, you'll then have to fit them. That's not too bad. The problem gets worse after that: you've got to balance the wheel on a rack so when it spins it doesn't wobble at all. That can be quite tricky. I mean, you're hardly starting from a perfect circle.'

He obviously understood bikes a lot better than she did. George frowned. 'But is there any alternative?'

Her new acquaintance mused silently for a moment. 'If it was my bike, I'd invest in a new wheel. And not the cheapest one in the shop, either. Bikes are like anything else. You get what you pay for.'

George sighed reluctantly. 'To be honest, I've ridden this

machine all through university. It was second hand – or probably much older – when I started. So I guess it doesn't owe me anything.'

She glanced over at what she presumed was the man's racing bike, its silver frame gleaming in the sun. 'Yours looks a strong bike. How much would one like that cost? And where do they sell them?'

'I'd be more than happy to answer those questions. But it'd take a few moments and it's not that comfortable crouching on the pavement. D'you reckon we could talk over a cup of coffee?'

Five minutes later they had taken a table in the window at the coffee shop opposite and the man had placed orders; their bikes were still visible over the road.

'There are all sorts of things to watch out for when choosing a new bike,' he began. 'You're not tall, so it mustn't be big or heavy. You'll need good-quality brakes and a wide range of gears. And, of course, a comfortable saddle.'

'Presumably your bike has all those things?'

He glanced across the road. 'That one's not mine, actually. But I've got one like it back in Bramston. Though mine's a bit more travelled.'

George smiled. You use it for your holidays, then?'

He laughed. 'I can't afford a car either. But if you're fit and healthy, as you and I are, a bike's all you need. This summer I cycled right through France and down to Italy. Without any problems at all. It's a well-made machine.' He took a sip of his coffee.

'I'm afraid I didn't use my bike at all. A girlfriend and I took a plane to Israel for the summer. That's an interesting place – lots of history. I don't suppose you've cycled that far?'

He laughed. 'They don't give me long enough off for that, I'm afraid.'

There was a short pause. He didn't add any more. But he had made George curious.

She frowned. 'Are you employed by a cycle manufacturer?'

'How did you know that?'

'Well, what else might you be doing with a second bike, just like your own?'

He considered her response. 'You're a clever woman. Good at deductions. Not a policewoman, I hope?'

'Not likely,' she replied. 'I'm a mathematician, actually. Training to be a business analyst.'

Another pause. 'So what is your job?' she continued. 'You keep contriving not to tell me.'

Cornered, he sighed. 'I'm into marketing. At present I'm trying to market racing bikes.'

It was sort of an explanation: enlightenment dawned. And with it came disappointment. 'That's the only reason you've brought me into this coffee shop? You see me as a potential customer?'

'To be precise, we're in here because you asked the question, "how much would a bike like mine cost?" We haven't even got far in answering. But I was rather enjoying the conversation. I do have other interests as well. My name's Mark, by the way. Mark Gilbert.'

'And I'm George. I was enjoying the conversation too. I hardly know anybody around here apart from my flatmates. Everyone in London seems so frantically busy.'

There was silence as they each drank more of their coffees. 'I could order us another,' he suggested.

'It's my turn to buy,' George replied. 'I'll get them shortly, I promise. First, though, I'd like to finish the topic of bikes. I obviously do need a new one. Today, preferably. I can afford to buy and I'm happy to take your advice. Tell me, where should I go?'

They managed to make their second coffees last another half hour. Then, leaving their bikes, they set out to catch a train for Hampstead.

'It's the best bike shop I know in North London,' Mark affirmed. 'They sell bikes like mine, ladies ones as well. And alternatives. You'll have a real choice. All the best bike makers are based on the Continent – there are lots more cyclists over there. And they've always got the Tour de France. Plus better weather, of course.'

George still hadn't learned exactly what Mark did, but now she wasn't wanting to talk about bikes. She wanted to make the most of her new friend. They had already identified a couple of new West End plays they hoped to enjoy together over the next few weeks by the time they reached the bike shop.

Mark was obviously well-known to the shop manager; he didn't need to ask where the top racing bikes were on display.

'Any one of these would be fine,' he affirmed as the pair stood facing the bike rack. 'Why don't I leave you to browse for half an hour. Then, if you fancy one, I'll have a word with the manager. I'm sure they'll let you take it for a ride.'

George had never bought a new bike before. The prices were higher than she'd expected, but still affordable; she was thankful she'd just received her first pay cheque. One bike had identical markings to the one Mark had been fiddling with, so she left that till last. When she came to check prices, she was surprised to find it was twenty percent cheaper than its competitors.

'I'd like to have a go on that one,' she told Mark, when he

rejoined her. He looked pleased at her choice and led her to the manager. Half an hour later she pushed the new machine out onto the street for a trial.

When she came back, George looked exultant. 'Mark, it's amazing. I didn't need to get off, even for the steepest hills; it goes like a dream. Yes, I'll take it.'

There was a further shock when she came to pay. For in her absence Mark had negotiated a further "supplier's discount" with the manager.

'Being knocked off my bike seemed like a terrible black cloud,' she told him, as they headed back to the station. 'But it's turned out to have a wonderful silver lining.'

'You mean, you've got a smart new bike?'

She turned toward him and smiled. 'No Mark. The bike's great, of course. What's really wonderful is that I've made a new friend.'

8   HENDERSONS' REVENGE

Sally Henderson had been left emotionally bruised by the Exchange evening at Howards. For her, being tickled was an integral part of lovemaking; but it had proved very different being tickled by a third party – even though Miles, her husband, had been present.

'Howard's a horrible man,' she told Miles with a shudder. 'I never want anything more to do with him.'

'It wasn't all down to him, Sally,' Miles remonstrated. 'After all, you were willing to take your dress off. Twice, as I understand it. Strictly speaking, he didn't force anything.'

Sally scowled. 'I'm not saying he's a physical bully but he's controlling. His immense skill is managing the wishes of others. Without him saying anything, it's clear what he wants. And hard not to go along with. I wish we could teach him a lesson.'

Miles could see his wife was upset. 'Trouble is, that isn't easy. Howard's a wealthy man; that gives him power. Whatever happens must never be associated with us. We're just a small firm of decorators. He'd wipe us out in a jiffy if it came to a battle of reputations.'

They struggled with alternate ideas.

'We're not after physical retaliation,' Miles concluded. 'Or mudslinging. We'd be bound to lose. Somehow or other we need to dent his reputation. But I've no idea how. We know so little about him.'

The project might have gone no further but for the spring

roadworks that led to special traffic lights along Harcourt Road.

Sally was driving to the shops when she was brought to a halt outside Howard's house. To her surprise she saw a woman coming out alone, fashionably dressed in an elegant suit.

Surprise! It didn't look like a cleaner. Even in Harcourt Road the best cleaners weren't this smart. Then Sally had an idea: was this the long spoken of "companion" who had been expected to return with Howard from Paris; had she finally arrived?

It was a three-lane junction. The lights persisted for ages on red, giving her time to ponder.

She was sure the woman hadn't been a guest at the Exchange evening. So she probably wasn't a friend.

A darker thought emerged. Was she here to audition? She had no idea what sort of films Howard was into, or how auditions might be conducted. Tickleability?

The lights finally turned green and Sally moved on. Either way, she mused, the woman must know more about Howard than she did.

Nothing more would have come of this except that, when she'd reached Sainsburys, she saw the woman was shopping here too. And by chance, when Sally reached the checkout, the mystery madam was just behind her.

She didn't usually accost total strangers, but this was too good an opportunity to miss.

'D'you happen to know Howard in Harcourt Road?' she asked, as they waited to be processed.

The woman looked surprised.

'I've just come from there. How d'you know him?'

The queue shuffled forwards, disrupting conversation.

Then:

'I'm part of the firm that helped decorate his house last summer.'

Obviously, for the woman, the claim rang some sort of bell. 'Ah, the crossed-paintbrush symbol? Have you time for a coffee?'

They found a quiet table in Sainsbury's café and ordered coffee. Then introduced themselves; the woman's name was Ursula.

'I'm Howard's secretary,' she explained. 'I'm normally in his office. An emergency brought me here.'

So she wasn't the mystery "companion" at all. Or even here to audition. They started their coffees.

'So you're the decorator,' beamed Ursula. 'Howard spoke highly of your work.'

Sally smiled. 'That's good news. We need happy customers.'

'Yes.' Then a doubt hit her. 'Mind, you weren't the lady who showed him round?'

Sally nodded, slightly apprehensive.

Ursula hesitated before she spoke. 'You made an unusual impression on Howard. He said you'd "strip for sixpence".' She frowned. 'I'm sure that couldn't be true.'

'I'm afraid it was. But it wasn't quite as it sounds. He led me into it.'

This was the acid test. She'd put her cards on the table: how would Ursula respond?

Her companion nodded. 'I feared it might be something like that. Howard's very persuasive; hard to resist.'

They'd reached the area Sally wanted to pursue. 'How do you cope with him, Ursula?'

Ursula sighed. 'Howard is fine in the office, with other people around. It's when I'm alone with him in Harcourt Road that there's a risk. You can imagine: I try like mad to avoid that happening.'

This was a precious exchange. Albeit ad-hoc. Sally had stumbled on an ally, but this might be the only chance she'd have to ask her questions.

'So what brings you here today, Ursula?'

Ursula grimaced. 'Howard phoned the office in a panic. Said he'd mislaid the key to his cellar office. That's where he keeps his private papers. Said he daren't come into the office and leave it unlocked. I had to come to him instead.'

'How had he contrived to lose it?'

'He'd had a party two days ago, swore one of the guests must have taken it. But of course he couldn't ask anybody without it sounding like an accusation. I asked him if it might be somewhere in the hall, but he wasn't having that. So I may have to keep coming here on my own – which, as you've found, is problematic. I wish I knew where it was.'

There was silence. Each finished their coffee and Sally made a decision. She brought an object from her handbag. 'Did it look anything like this?'

The encounter moved to an Indian restaurant. The conversation now needed to be really secret; and had also made them hungry. They took a table away from the window and placed their orders.

'So how'd you get this?'

Sally smiled. 'My husband and I were first to the party. I was cajoled into being tickled remorselessly in Howard's low-ceiling cellar. It was pretty grim. Then, once I'd redressed, I was sent to answer the door to welcome later guests, while the men tidied themselves up downstairs. I was feeling bruised, saw the cellar key on my way up and grabbed it – some instinct told me it might be useful. The question now, Ursula, is how?'

Ursula pondered for a while.

'It shouldn't be too hard for me to "find" this key in the hallway. He's got plenty of furniture and a wide range of ornaments. But first . . . shouldn't we take a copy?'

'I already have. I keep it in my bedside drawer.'

Ursula smiled. 'Good work. There are lots of documents in that office that could destroy Howard. Copies of his tax returns, for example. I never pry. . . but I suspect the worst.'

'Are you ever left in there on your own?'

Ursula shook her head. 'Sally, I'm a private secretary: Howard's employee. I'd move on but he pays me well. If there was ever the remotest suspicion that I had removed any of his documents, he wouldn't just fire me. I'd be hung, drawn and quartered.'

'Metaphorically speaking, I hope?'

'Well, that office does have a soundproof ceiling. I'm not taking the risk.'

'In any case,' she continued, 'the ending would be sticky. His reference would ensure that no-one would ever employ me again. No, we need to be a lot more subtle.'

They paused and began eating their biryanis.

'Mind, he's often away on business trips.'

Sally bit into her naan bread and nodded encouragingly.

'I do have an emergency front door key,' conceded Ursula. 'I guess I could get an extra copy made.'

A rough plan was forming. More curry was consumed.

'I manage Howard's diary,' she reflected. 'I could alert you when I knew he'd be abroad. He relies on that cellar key, never locks his desk.'

'Ah. You mean, I could come in at night and ransack his office. Send the contents straight to the media. And wait for something to emerge.'

For a few seconds the idea sounded brilliant. Then cold reality intervened.

'Trouble is, Ursula, I'm not a habitual burglar. I might get caught. Even if I wore gloves. Howard probably has security operating when he's away. Cameras, for instance. That'd be deadly. He'd recognise me, you see – and he knows where to find me. My fate would be much like yours. Miles and I would never paint again. Except possibly in prison.'

Unless they could find a professional burglar to do the job on their behalf, it seemed they were stumped. There was a gloomy silence as they continued their meal.

'Good day, dear?' asked Miles cheerfully, when Sally returned home.

'Manageable,' she replied. It was probably best not to divulge her lunchtime conversation. 'And you?'

'I had an idea about Howard. I'd got his full name from our decorating contract. I knew I'd never get his tax details or anything. But he's into films; and films always need viewers. If he had anything to display, he would need publicity. So I searched for his name on the internet.'

'Right.' Typical of the resourceful Miles, she thought, to think further ahead.

'Yes. Turns out, he's not into dark films at all. His niche is much more mundane. He advertises petfood.'

Sally was gobsmacked; her jaw dropped.

'You mean – all he wanted my colour coordination skills for was to create a backdrop that viewers would find desirable, as the dog munched away.'

57

'That's right. Much less grand. But knowing that gives us a mighty strong card – that's, of course, if we ever rub shoulders with Howard again.'

Harcourt Road, Sheffield. A busy, thriving street, backing onto a park and lake

9 COMPETITIVE AND TENDER

Harriet owned a small farm on the Sussex Downs. Young runners would be sent to her for training with little risk they'd be
distracted. 'We'll do our best with anyone,' she said. Marsden
Farm was ten miles north of Chichester and (unlike North,
East and West Marsden) miles from a village. There was little
here except the South Downs Way.

Steve, just out of school and as thin as a whippet, had been
sent along by Brighton Harriers. 'The lad's got great potential,'
they said. 'It needs to be ruthlessly developed.'

'Right, young man,' said Harriet when Steve arrived, having
walked in from the twice-a-week bus stop with a heavy rucksack, 'I've been told to give you the toughest fortnight of your
life. Up at six for a cold shower, then a long run on the Downs
before breakfast. Mind, when you get back, you can have as
much bacon and eggs as you fancy. I don't want you losing any
weight.'

There was little risk of Harriet dieting, thought Steve. She
waddled rather than walked. He wondered how much she
weighed. No doubt running the farm kept her exercised. She
didn't seem to have any helpers – perhaps the place was too
remote?

'After that,' she said, 'and a break – you can use it to help
me stack bales in you like – I'll send you out again. Same process, different location, in the afternoon. But at the end of the
day you – and anyone else they send along – can join in one of
my famous farmhouse suppers.'

'The plan is, you'll run each day to the same locations, and I'll time you. There are plenty of ups and downs.' She gave a chuckle which Steve (mistakenly) took to be supportive. 'But you'd better improve over time, lad, or you'll be missing some of your supper.'

Next morning the regime began. Steve was mustard keen and his opening times on the two runs seemed to satisfy Harriet. By evening he was dog tired. There was just him and Harriet to share a massive supper.

'Aren't you a bit lonely here, Harriet?' he asked. 'Or are all your workers on holiday?'

Harriet shook her head. 'No, there's just me. I'm too busy to be lonely. I don't need a phone – even if I could get one fitted out here. There's a call box in North Marsden for emergencies. How about you?'

'I'm a bit of a loner,' Steve confessed. 'I've not been much good at anything except running. That's why I want to push myself as far as I can.'

'Well, your opening times today were excellent. Let's see how much you can improve them.'

The first week passed in a companionable way. Steve wanted to be helpful and found plenty of ways to assist Harriet on the farm; also, his run times improved steadily.

One day another athlete arrived, brought by his father from Sheffield.

'I'm Sebastian,' he introduced himself. 'But I'd prefer you to call me "Baz".'

Baz oozed self-confidence and had far more running gear: Steve noticed he'd come with spiked running shoes and a bespoke stopwatch. And a plan. He was far from happy when

Harriet wanted him on the same training runs as Steve.

'My dad knows these parts,' he asserted. 'He tells me it's possible to run along the South Downs Way almost as far as Petersfield.'

'It certainly is,' Harriet told him. 'For an experienced marathon runner. But that's not you. To start with, on day one, I want you on exactly the same route as Steve. That way I can directly compare you.'

It was clear that Baz didn't like this, but Harriet was adamant.

Steve hoped the two might be able to run together; he would be glad of company over the Downs. There was no sign, though, of Baz when he set off next morning. It turned out his fellow-athlete had set off even earlier.

Harriet wasn't going to cook breakfasts at two different times. Baz had to wait, which didn't please him. Harriet, though, was used to awkward customers and ignored him.

'There's not much between you,' she said cheerfully as she served their cooked breakfasts. 'Steve was a minute faster, but he's done that run several times before. Tomorrow you'd better start together. That way you can egg each other on.'

The notion that he wasn't the fastest runner on the farm seemed a shock to Baz. But it did motivate him to run alongside Steve in future. He wouldn't be beaten again.

And as Harriet knew, the competition (if not the intense rivalry) was good for both of them.

Even though they ran together they didn't like one another. They were too different to be natural soulmates.

Steve came from a humble background in a Brighton suburb. No-one in his family had ever run in their lives – except, occasionally, to catch a bus. They couldn't understand his running ambitions at all.

Whereas Baz came from a long ancestry of Sheffield runners. His father had run for Yorkshire and no doubt hoped his son would do the same. He even wrote him letters of encouragement.

Today they'd achieved a dead heat on their early morning run. Harriet was amazed, not by their simultaneous arrival back at the farm, but by the speed with which they'd reached it.

'These are the best times I've ever had from young athletes training at my farm,' she declared. 'If you stick at it, one day you might both be Olympians. We haven't had a successful middle-distance runner since Roger Bannister in the 1950s. That was twenty years ago.'

The next day, encouraged, the athletes set out to run even faster.

Harriet didn't explain how the post office had managed to deliver anything to her remote farm, but there was a letter waiting for Baz on their return. He opened it over breakfast, quickly skimmed it but made no comment on who it was from.

After breakfast the letter was left it open while he went to brush his teeth and Steve couldn't help but glance at it. What caught his attention was a whole series of times and distances. He guessed these must be intended to help Baz fine-tune his pacing over the various stages of a race. That was looking well ahead. The missive was from "Peter"; Steve guessed that must be his father.

It was nothing more than a casual glance. Nothing would have come of it except that Baz came back into the dining room to pick it up and saw his rival near it. And was incandescent.

'Spying on my private correspondence, Steve. These are clues as to how I'll race in the future. I'm shocked. They're no business of yours. It's outrageous.'

Steve could see how upset he was. 'I'm sorry, Baz. I didn't read any of it, I just thought it looked intriguing. I wish my family took more interest in my running. You're very fortunate.'

Later they ran once again, starting together. This time, though, there was no friendly chatter between them.

The afternoon run ended with a furious sprint through the farmyard, which ended in a dead heat.

But once they'd go their breath back, they were disturbed to see no sign of Harriet and her stopwatch waiting for them.

Baz noted their times on his own watch. 'Steve, I reckon that's half a minute faster than yesterday. Harriet will be delighted.'

But right now Steve's attention was elsewhere. Harriet had always been waiting at the door. Something was wrong.

He pushed into the farm kitchen. She'd been there recently enough, preparing their evening meal: potato peel in the colander and a shepherd's pie in the aga.

Baz was worried too, strode past him into the dining room. There came a call.

'Steve. Harriet's here, on the floor. I think she might be dead.'

Steve rushed through. The woman was on the floor, arms askew, a look of intense pain on her face. She wasn't moving at all.

He recalled some rudimentary first aid, knelt down and felt for her pulse.

'She's still alive, Baz. Just. But we need an ambulance –

quickly.'

'How on earth are we going to do that, Steve? There's no phone here; even the nearest neighbour is miles away.'

Steve pondered for a second. 'One of us needs to run back along the South Downs Way till it crosses that main road. Then hitch a lift to the nearest callbox and ring 999.'

Baz nodded. 'OK. I'll do that. Can you stay here with Harriet? Make sure she's kept as warm as possible.'

It was an age before help arrived. Steve sat beside Harriet and held her hand, whispering words of comfort. Then a moment of relief as he saw the flashing lights of an ambulance in the farmyard.

The crew rushed in, holding a stretcher. Five minutes later Harriet was on her way to Chichester Hospital.

'Will she survive?' he asked.

'There's a chance,' was the best the crewman could offer.

Steve was still recovering his equilibrium when Baz's taxi arrived from Chichester.

The two swapped notes, their earlier animosity lost in the current crisis.

'We've done our best, Baz.'

'And shown we can work together after all. Even though we are competitors. Hey Steve, would you like to see my dad's advice on pacing a race?'

10   THE BLACK HOLE

'There's something wrong with this scorecard,' said Greg, as his golf partner returned from the Red Lion bar, carrying two foaming pints of Henley's bitter.

'You mean, it shows I won?' replied Laurie, grinning cheerfully as he sat down. 'I did have a few surprising putts towards the end, you know.'

'Not that. Count them: our scores are only recorded for seventeen holes.'

Laurie grabbed the card and peered at it. 'We probably forgot to write anything down for the tenth. That was when the rain started pelting down, remember. And you realised you'd not brought your waterproof.' He shrugged. 'Let's just assume we took five strokes each. I still won. Cheers.'

Greg sipped his drink but frowned; his equilibrium had been disturbed. 'Trouble is, I don't remember actually playing that hole. We might have missed it out completely.'

'We can come here again next week. We'll follow the "next tee" signs more carefully. I'm sure there's not a course in the whole country that's got just seventeen holes.'

They returned a week later and played the course again. It was true: there was no tenth hole. Or at least, not one that they found. The "next tee" sign beside the ninth green led them straight on to the start of the eleventh.

There was a trio of zealous ladies following close behind them, so they hadn't time to look further. It made no difference to their enjoyment of the round – Laurie won again – but it was rather puzzling.

'How can a golf course "lose" one of its holes?' asked Laurie, as they enjoyed another well-earned lunch in the Red Lion. 'I mean, all the signs were clear. It's been deliberately omitted from the standard round.'

'And it's a decent enough course in other respects. Their Clubhouse is rather posh – too posh for us, anyway. They're not short of money. Someone wealthy is behind it.'

Greg mused for a moment. 'I can see only two possibilities. Either the tenth hole never existed at all. Or else it was there once; and for some reason or other it's been abandoned.'

Laurie reflected on the options as he sipped his beer. 'If it doesn't exist at all, it would be interesting to know why.'

He mused for a moment. 'Whoever designed the course must have planned to have eighteen holes.' He paused. 'Hey. Maybe the land they'd planned to buy and use for the tenth hole was lost – say, to a builder, who put in a higher offer for that bit of land.'

Greg saw where he was going. 'Perhaps the guy was building an estate nearby, needed more space to lay it all out?'

'You mean, he was after higher profits?'

Greg was doubtful. 'Could that work? As we said earlier, the Club seems fairly wealthy.'

There was some cogitation, then Laurie voiced a suggestion.

'Maybe the Club wasn't so wealthy when it began, and was outbid?'

'But Laurie, they could have offered something else besides money. Life membership to the builder, say. Or if he didn't like golf, to the owners of the estate properties. That would certainly help him sell his new houses.'

At that point their haddock and chips were brought and the golfers focussed attention on their meals. But they were still wrestling silently with the mystery of the missing hole.

'The alternative to the Club never owning the land, Greg, is that there once was a tenth hole; then something dreadful happened which caused them to close it down for ever.'

Greg finished his mouthful before he replied. 'It would have to be something very dramatic to make that happen. What d'you suggest?'

Laurie laid down his cutlery and pondered, sipping his beer for inspiration. 'Well, what if someone died on the tenth green? Maybe . . . they had a heart attack?'

He pursued the idea. 'What if they were as shocked as you or I would be, as they sank a long-range putt? So the tenth was the last hole they ever played.'

Greg smiled at the thought. 'It'd be a magnificent way to go. A lot better than dying of old age.'

'Even better if it was the eighteenth hole, Greg. He'd have completed the round.'

The wild idea appealed to both for a few moments. Then Greg voiced his reservations.

'Isn't it rare for anyone to die on a golf course? They wouldn't be playing on their own. Their partner would call an ambulance and they'd be hauled off to hospital. Maybe airlifted – they're miles from the road here. Unless his death was registered as "occurred on the tenth hole", there'd be no good reason for the Club to close it for ever.'

'But if something like that had happened – even if he'd died in despair after missing a six- inch putt – I could imagine his family might want to commission a memorial at the hole.'

Greg shook his head. 'In that case, Laurie, they'd surely

want the hole left open, so regular golfers would be reminded of the hazards of golf every time they played.' He shook his head. 'I don't think it can be that simple.'

By now they'd finished the main meal but hadn't solved the problem. 'Let's have a dessert. Put our diets on hold.' Treacle sponge and custard was ordered, and more beer. This might take some time.

As Laurie went to the toilet, Greg consulted his smartphone.

Yes, the golf course was on here. It had its own website, with a potted history. He started to browse.

'The course dated from the last century,' he told Laurie when he returned. 'It almost went bankrupt. But it was rescued five years ago by two Japanese brothers, Kenji and Haruki, who worked in the City. No wonder the place seems so wealthy.'

'But what on earth has this got to do with the missing hole?'

Their conversation stopped as their desserts arrived. Then Laurie ventured a theory.

'Sometimes brothers in business fall out. Are they joint owners?'

Greg consulted his phone and studied the potted history. It was not encyclopaedic, gave names but few details.

He tried entering the owners' names into Google directly.

'Well, here's one of 'em,' he said. 'Kenji gets a whole article to himself. The golf club is hardy mentioned. It's mainly his interest in Japanese politics.'

'OK. What about the other one - Haruki?'

Greg stopped eating to search harder. He frowned.

'I can't find a mention anywhere. Perhaps he died.'

Laurie smiled triumphantly. 'OK. How about this for an idea. What if the two owners were playing golf and had a fierce argument. Maybe on the tenth hole.'

Greg considered. 'Or else they had a dreadful accident. Perhaps Haruki was impatient, completed his drive, walked forward before Kenji had driven off. When he did so the shot was wayward and hit Haruki on the head.'

Laurie concurred. 'After all, we don't know they were skilled golfers. They might have been as bad as us.'

Greg continued. 'In either case, Laurie, if Haruki was killed, what came next? Remember, Kenji would now own the whole course. That would give him a lot of power over the staff working there.'

Laurie saw where he was going. 'Let's assume the two were playing in the autumn. No one else around. Kenji might be strongly motivated to keep the whole incident quiet – he certainly wouldn't want to bring it to the attention of the police.'

'And after all, they were brothers, Laurie, living abroad. Maybe in the same house. It might be wise to dampen down enquiries. He could suggest, say, that Haruki had "gone home" and shelter in the double entrendre.'

There was a pause then Laurie asked the killer question. 'OK. But even if he did, Kenji would still need to get rid of his brother's body.'

There was a longer silence but now both men were excited. They ate more of their desserts.

'You know, Laurie, that golf course has some really deep bunkers. We've each been in several today. What if Kenji managed to bury his brother in one – say, one close to the tenth green?'

Laurie nodded. 'Yes. That would certainly give him good

reason to ban the tenth hole from all future use. As owner he could ensure that happened.'

It was a shocking idea, but not totally implausible.

After they'd finished their meal, they strode up to the bar to settle the bill.

'You wuz 'aving a long discussion,' observed the landlord, as he handed them the card machine.

'We were intrigued by something on the local golf course,' said Greg. 'We were playing there this morning, you see.'

The landlord checked the payment had gone through and nodded. 'Ah. You mean the Black Hole?' It sounded like he'd guessed the nub of their problem.

'So you've played there too?'

'A long time ago. My back's not too good these days. But it's still doing well, I gather?'

Laurie nodded. Then he asked for follow up. 'So what's your theory of the Black Hole?'

'Ain't just a theory, sir. I know.'

'Go on then.'

'Well, the course wuz rescued by two Japanese entrepreneurs. They wuz keen golfers but not much good. But both were knowledgeable gardeners. One day they spotted Japanese knotweed on the tenth hole. It's a deadly plant, very hard to remove once it's taken hold. They daren't risk it spreading across the rest of the course.

'So they went back to the clubhouse and issued the order: the tenth hole was out of bounds until the knotweed was all removed. I gather that they are still working on the problem.'

11   OVER THE LINE

Sally and Miles Henderson's long-standing policy – "we only charge when the job's finished" – had been severely tested by the Sunset Care Home. When they won the contract to redecorate the whole Home, it had seemed a windfall: cosy indoor work for several winter weeks. Sally even agreed a striking lemon and lime colour scheme with the Home's management that would apply across every room.

But management couldn't remove all the residents and leave the place empty. They had to rely on holidays, hospital visits and the occasionally death to leave individual rooms vacant for a few days. When that happened, the deal was they would call in the painters at short notice.

The whole project dragged on for months. Miles was philosophical, fine-tuning his accounting regime in between other projects, but the feisty Sally grew ever less patient.

The Home was a hundred years old. It had forty residents, living on two floors, plus a lounge, dining room, treatment room and office, as well as stairs, a lift and corridors. The common spaces were not too difficult: the Hendersons brought along flood lights and tackled these one by one, mostly at night. A few residents wandered about in the small hours, but the decorators managed to shepherd them away from repainted surfaces. Or else persuade them that 'touching new lemon paint was an omen of bad luck'.

Gradually the rooms were decorated. In the end there was

just one left, at the far end of the upstairs corridor; it belonged to "Rita".

Neither Miles nor Sally knew what Rita looked like. They might have encountered her in the lounge, but they hadn't picked up residents' names – they weren't that diligent. So Rita's room was unpainted; and the decorating bill was unsent.

Eventually the call came. 'Rita's gone away. Can you come this morning?'

Miles had disappeared the day before on some mystery or other, but Sally was only too pleased to oblige. She donned her painting overall, gathered her gear and headed for the Home. There she was given the spare key for Rita's room and left to get on with it. Speed was essential; she hadn't been told how long Rita would be away.

Sally felt relief: she was inside the room at last. Rita certainly wasn't the tidiest woman on the planet. Her room was a tip; she hadn't even cleared her desk. But Sally was ready for that. She had several large plastic boxes and bundled the loose items into one or other, noting the location for each. The contents of the bookshelf went into another. She couldn't get into the locked wardrobe, but she told herself that didn't have to be painted.

Maybe, she thought, the disarray had been due to Rita's sudden departure.

The rooms at the rear of the Home each had a balcony. She didn't intend to paint this at all so could leave the container boxes outside. Fortunately it wasn't expected to rain.

Lastly, she covered all the floor and furniture with protective sheets: now the decorating could begin.

The room hadn't been painted for decades. The ceiling might once have been magnolia but was now a grubby cream.

Sally wondered if Rita was a secret smoker.

There was also a great deal of dark paint on the mantelpiece, bookshelves and panels. On the agreed colour scheme all these surfaces were going to become light lemon. Sally could see no alternative but to remove the dark paint completely before she began to paint.

Amongst her equipment was an old absinthe bottle which now contained a fiercer version of "Nitromors", the well-known paint remover. Version one was almost as old as the Home itself, toxic in taste, touch and smell. It had to be handled with care.

First Sally propped open the door onto the balcony. It was cold but she needed as much fresh air as possible. Then, donning safety goggles and thick gloves, she started work, coating each dark surface in turn. The smell was horrific and she had to go out onto the balcony several times to recover, while the Nitromors caused the dark paint to peel off. But the various surfaces needed several coats to remove it all. It took her the whole day to complete this phase of the work.

Miles wasn't back when she got home. She seized the chance to have a long, bubbly bath to wash the smells away; and a leisurely supper.

Next day she was back early at the Home.

Sally wondered, as she climbed up and down her stepladder, sugar-soaping and then painting the ceiling, what Rita was like? Of course, that didn't affect the painting itself, but she preferred to have a relationship with her clients. Was the woman friendly or was she a recluse? She certainly didn't seem to go away often. But she must have wealth from somewhere, to be living here for years on end? The Sunset Home wasn't cheap.

It was as she stepped down, feeling pleased that at last she'd finished the ceiling's first coat, that Sally was shocked to realise there was a mysterious figure standing on the balcony.

'Hello,' she said cautiously, as she unlocked the balcony door.

It was a middle-aged man, casually dressed, wearing a fleece.

'I'm sorry to disturb you,' he said. 'My name's Francis – Francis Rutherford. I was hoping to catch Rita.'

'By climbing onto her private balcony?'

'She's an elusive woman. This Home is very protective of its residents. I asked at the main entrance but Rita's left word that she doesn't want visitors, so they wouldn't let me in.'

'Or to put it another way, you shouldn't be here at all.' Sally was aware that she needed to protect her hirer's privacy.

Francis smiled. 'I was leaving out the back when I spotted movement inside her room. I assumed it must be Rita. So I shinned up the fire escape that's been so thoughtfully added to each balcony.'

'But she's not here, Francis. I'm very busy, decorating her room while she's away.'

Sally did her best to present the statement as a dismissal, but the man was determined.

'Can I try to explain?' he pleaded.

Sally didn't trust him but she was curious. 'I'll give you five minutes. Then I'll have to get on. And whatever happens, I'm certainly not letting you inside.'

They perched themselves on the plastic boxes and a conversation began.

'My interest in Rita is that she may owe us a great deal of

74

tax. I'm a tax-recovery agent for Inland Revenue.'

Sally, though no tax enthusiast, was sceptical. 'You might do better chasing top businessmen like, say, Jeff Bezos. He probably owes this country billions. Why don't you climb onto his balcony?'

'I can authenticate myself.' Francis protested. He reached inside his fleece and produced various papers, which he handed over.

Sally looked through them. She was no tax expert, but they looked genuine enough. Even so, she was still suspicious. She handed them back.

'But if Rita really has a big tax bill, that should be settled in the courts, shouldn't it?'

He nodded. 'Yes, in the last resort. But there are complications which I'm afraid I can't explain to a third party. A direct appeal to Rita might have more impact.'

Sally glanced at her watch. There was no way she could take this any further. 'Well, I'm sorry Francis. I'm afraid I can't help you. Now I have to get on.'

She watched him turn and climb slowly back down the fire escape, then returned to her painting.

When Sally got home that evening, she was pleased to see that Miles had returned.

'So where've you been?' she asked, as they started their supper.

'Background research on Rita Rutherford.'

Sally blinked. 'Tell me more.'

'Well, it occurred to me that the Home must have details of next of kin for each resident. So I applied a bit of pressure and got Rita's details. Her closest relative is a younger sister, Tessa, who's married and lives in Norfolk. I rang her, outlined our connection to her sister and got invited down to meet her. Then, after I'd explained our problem, Tessa rang Rita. That's how the pair of us got Rita out of the Home.'

'Right. Very clever. But why on earth is Rita so reclusive?'

Miles smiled. He liked being asked questions which he could answer. 'Well. It turns out she was married for years. Her husband was very wealthy but also a controlling bully. In the end she walked out on him and they battled through a long and bitter divorce. The final settlement is what keeps paying for Rita's room in the Home.'

That was the financial mystery explained, anyway.

'Alright. I suppose that might explain why she's so reclusive.' Then a thought hit her. 'Hold on, Miles, did you say her name was Rutherford?'

'Yes. Why?'

'I met someone else called Rutherford today. At the Home.' Sally outlined the incident which had started when Francis climbed up onto Rita's balcony.

'But it's too much of a coincidence,' she said, 'that they are both called Rutherford. D'you reckon that Francis is really her controlling ex-husband, who's still trying to assert control?'

It was a good question. They pondered as they continued eating.

'If it is him, Miles, that raises another question. It surely beggars belief that, after all this time, he appeared here on the very day after she'd gone away to stay with her sister.'

Miles mused for a moment and then nodded. 'The only way I can account for that is that, somehow or other, Francis had been keeping tabs on Tessa. So when he heard Rita was coming there, he knew she'd be away and headed straight up for the Sunset Home.'

'Trouble is, Sally, now he's found out where Rita is living, he can easily go back again, climb onto her balcony, break in and ransack her room. You've confirmed to him which one it is.'

Sally wasn't that put out and smiled. 'You know, I had a suspicion there was something odd about him. His answers were all far too slick. So I took one precaution that should discourage him.'

'Oh yes?'

'I had the bottle of the old Nitromors with me. So before I left this evening, I liberally coated the balcony rail, the top of the fire escape and the outside balcony door handle. If Francis decides to come back in the next few days to search Rita's room, he's going to be in for a nasty shock.'

12   LOST IN THE BUNKER

Shouldering their golf bags, Laurie and Greg trudged down the lane. But at the golf club reception they were surprised to see a notice on the door: "Closed for the Day". No explanation was offered.

'Doesn't affect folk like us, I think,' said Greg optimistically.

'Serendipity,' agreed his companion. 'I can try out my new camera without the bother of paying.'

Laurie had been sent the device by his sister. He was slightly disconcerted, though, by the accompanying note: 'To the most boring man on the planet. Please, darling, take up a new hobby.'

There was no-one else in sight as they headed for the first tee.

'Right Greg. What I'd like is for you to film my drive. I know it's not right – never has been. Maybe if we can film it and then watch it in slow motion, I can see what's wrong.'

Greg was happy to oblige. In truth, his drive was no better. They'd both had lessons on the club's driving range, but it hadn't made much difference.

The camera was set up on a tripod, focussed on Laurie, and the process began.

The golfer swung his driver above shoulder height and had a practice swing. Then he repeated the exercise several times, his face contorting with the effort.

'If you could do it like and also hit the ball, Laurie, it might work well.'

It might. But of course it didn't happen. Laurie swung hard but this time topped his ball, which wobbled apologetically off the tee. Greg had captured the event on video, but it wasn't one his friend would want to dwell on. Successful drives were what he was after.

It was as the process was repeated for perhaps the tenth time that Greg was conscious of a sound behind him, the other side of a nearby thick hedge.

'Ow. That hurts, Benedict.'

It was a female voice. Now their golf course went back and forth. Greg knew the tenth hole ran along behind the hedge, with the green at this end; but whoever was over there wasn't occupied with golf.

He frowned at Laurie; the two continued to listen in silence.

The voice again. 'I really don't like lying on my back on this sand, Benedict. Why don't we swap round? You lie down and I'll sit astride you.'

There was silence, apart from the scuffles arising from the interchange.

As they waited, Greg pointed to the camera and then at the hedge. The squeeze was probably consensual. Even so, they'd better not ignore it.

Laurie saw what he was suggesting and nodded. Between them they arranged for the camera to focus through the foliage onto the tenth-green bunker. They knew exactly where that lay: they regularly visited it on their weekly rounds.

'Keira, there's a camera on us from behind that hedge. The production crew shouldn't be here yet.'

'Maybe they need more rehearsal. Why don't I strip off completely? Give them something to focus on.'

The man laughed. 'I'm not going to stop you. What happens after that?'

There was silence. Perhaps the woman saw no need to answer.

Greg gestured questioningly to Laurie. They were hardly official visitors. Whatever was happening was not their business. Quietly the camera was taken down and the two headed for another hole.

It was two hours later before the puzzled golfers learned any more. They had been working round the course, filming each other's drives with limited success, when on the twelfth tee they came upon more action.

Two hundred yards away, a bunch of cameramen surrounded the green. They were coordinated by a director armed with a loudhailer, sitting in a buggy. On the green, clutching their putters, were two actors who looked vaguely familiar. They were engaged in a monstrous row.

The lads had seen one of them before. It was the woman whom they had heard complaining and had filmed undressing on the tenth green: Keira. Now, though, she was fully clothed and dressed for golf.

The other looked faintly familiar too, but he certainly wasn't the man they'd seen before, Benedict. Nowhere near tall enough. But he still looked extremely rugged. Laurie started to realise what his sister had meant: he was rather out of touch, in a private world of his own.

'I believe that's Tom Cruise,' murmured his golfing partner, sensing his uncertainty. 'He's the most famous film star on the planet. I reckon we've barged in on a snippet of top-grade film production.' Something clicked. 'Hey, Laurie - that must be why the course is closed.'

But before they could say any more, they were addressed by the director on his megaphone.

'We need a couple of extras over here,' he bellowed. 'Would you mind helping us?'

'What d'you want us to do?' shouted back Greg.

'Walk towards us down the fairway. Then, very politely, ask our two so-called golfers here why they're not moving on. Tell 'em it's holding up your play. What will happen next is unscripted: let them tell you in their own words. But we'll film the whole scene and then decide how much to keep.'

They'd never had such an invitation before – and they never would again. If they'd been given a month to steady their nerves, it would have ruined the whole thing. But as it was, they only had to play themselves.

'Try to look like you're enjoying yourself,' muttered Greg, as the pair set off down the fairway. He kept smiling as they approached the green. Maybe a few minutes of fame – a tiny part on a major film – would silence Laurie's sister?

In fact it was Laurie who spoke first.

'I don't know what's the matter with you two,' he began. 'There are plenty of places in life for a couple to have rows, but a putting green isn't one of them.'

'Whatever the problem, you shouldn't stop two old lags like Laurie and me having our morning round,' added Greg.

The actors were obviously slightly shaken by the brusque comments. Tom was the first to respond.

'Keira and I are meant to be celebrating our anniversary. We've been together for two whole years. But we've just realised that she's lost her engagement ring.'

'I'm sure I had it on when we set out,' wailed Keira. 'I must have lost it on the way round.'

'It's not that easy to lose a ring, surely,' asked Laurie the

81

innocent. 'Assuming it was well-fitted, of course.'

'Might you have lost it in a bunker?' added his friend.

Tom turned to his actor-partner. 'That's it! You spent ages in that bunker two holes back. I bet it's in there somewhere. We'd better go back and look.'

'There's a short-cut through to the tenth green over here,' said the ever-helpful Laurie.

'Wait a minute, Keira,' said Tom. 'You weren't even in that bunker. By some miracle that was the one time you landed on the green.'

Keira stamped her feet, looking at him with contempt. 'These . . . these sand pits, they all look the same to me. It's a ridiculous game. How can anyone take it seriously?'

Listening to her words, Laurie was shocked. He'd never heard such dreadful sentiments in his whole life. He had to intervene.

'But you've been in the tenth bunker at least once, Keira,' he observed.

'Nonsense.'

But this woman had damned his beloved game. And the remit he'd been given by the director was to "be himself". Laurie reached for his beloved camera.

'I captured it on film,' he said. 'Look here.'

'Hold on a minute,' said the director, sensing an unexpected breakthrough. 'I think we all need to see this.' He took the camera from Laurie and plugged it into the large screen mounted on his buggy.

'It was half past eight this morning,' recalled Greg. 'It was my idea to film it.' He didn't want Laurie taking all the credit.

Laurie fiddled with his camera, reversed past shot after shot of two hapless golfers fluffing their drives. Finally he reached the first tee; and the overheard conversation on the tenth.

Tom and Keira looked on in genuine amazement. This hadn't been in the script.

For it was certainly Keira. She stood in the tenth-green bunker, removing every stitch of clothing. But the man enjoying the view certainly wasn't Tom; it was someone else altogether.

When the clip was over, Tom looked shocked. 'I'm not sure I can take this, Keira. I knew Benedict was a friend of yours, but I didn't realise he was that kind of friend. No wonder you lost your engagement ring.' A thought struck him. 'Hey, can you play this scene again, but this time in slow motion?'

Laurie had never tried slow-mo, but the director had. This time they saw the ring fall into the sand. And then Benedict seize it. It was hard evidence in a world of make-believe.

Afterwards it took Greg some time to persuade Laurie that the whole thing was only a film, probably a romantic comedy. It wasn't reality.

'Laurie, we spent the morning among actors. World-famous people like Tom Cruise and Keira Knightly. But at least it'll give you something to tell your sister,' he concluded.

'Trouble is,' said Laurie gloomily, 'I've never heard of any of 'em.'

Greg sighed. 'Your sister is right. You do need to get out more. We'll make sure we go to see the film when it's been released.'

13 LOVEJOY'S ANTIQUES

This must be the place, thought Maurice. It wasn't busy, anyway. He stepped into the gloomy premises. They weren't spending much money on lighting. Should that be taken as a plus or a minus?

Lovejoy was in the back room but emerged at the welcome sound of a customer.

'Good morning, sir. Can I help you?'

'I hope so,' he replied. 'It's my mantelpiece clock. It's started to go slow.'

So saying, he reached inside his backpack and produced a beautiful gold-plated timepiece that looked a good hundred years old.

Lovejoy shook his head. 'I'm sorry, sir. I'm no mechanic.'

'But you supplied it.'

'I don't think so. We haven't met before.'

'I'm Maurice Minor, from Waddesdon Manor. I sent my man for it. There can't be that many "Lovejoy Antiques" in Wantage.'

They exchanged alternate lines in a tense dialogue. Eventually a stumped Lovejoy felt he'd been trapped and had to take action of some sort.

'Alright sir. Let me take a look.'

The customer placed the clock carefully on the polished counter and stood back.

Lovejoy hadn't actually taken any antiques to pieces in his latest career, but it couldn't be that difficult. He reminded himself, whatever he was feeling, to look confident. He had to take his customer with him.

'It's certainly a beautiful object, sir.'

There was an embossed Greek symbol on the face which made no sense at all. Lovejoy turned the timepiece round. Then he spotted a catch which clicked open the back. Now he could see various pieces of machinery – interlocking toothed wheels and, lower down, a well-wound spring – but what might be going wrong?

On one side was a small escapement, bouncing steadily back and forth. He guessed that controlled the rate at which the device ran. But there was no obvious way to speed it up.

This was a performance with a live audience: he reminded himself that he needed to keep talking. He was about to ask how much the clock was worth when he remembered: as an antique specialist, he ought to have at least as much idea as his customer.

In desperation he picked it up for a closer look.

'It's extremely delicate,' warned Maurice.

'And quite heavy,' he responded. He was tempted to flip it in the air just to watch the expression of horror on Maurice's face but managed to restrain himself. He hadn't yet secured insurance for accidents on the premises. Which reminded him, someone was due to come about that shortly.

Now it was in his hands, the object seemed heavier than he'd have expected. His fingers felt underneath. There was something inside the base: a rectangular plastic box. That surely couldn't be a hundred years old?

He was about to ask the customer what it was, but some instinct restrained him. He didn't want to risk embarrassment.

'Could you leave it with me for a day or two, sir? I'd like to check how quickly it loses time; and see how the loss rate varies over the day.'

Maurice was hardly enthusiastic, but he couldn't reasonably refuse. He nodded slowly, seized his backpack and headed for the door.

As he left the shop a second person entered.

'Good morning,' the woman said. 'I'm Irene Tempest. I 'm here to talk about insurance.'

'Ah, thank you for coming, Irene. I'm Lovejoy. My problem is assessing the value of my shop's antique contents. Most of them were sold to me along with the shop, so I'm not sure how to rate them.'

Irene looked business-like. 'Before we get onto that, Lovejoy, I'd like to ask you a few questions. First of all, when you bought and, I assume, renamed this shop, did you have any doubts about your predecessor?'

'He was eager to sell, Irene. I happened to see the advert one day in the Wantage Gazette and I was tempted. I'd just retired, you see, was after a new project, and this looked ideal. Seemed like the last owner couldn't get away quick enough.'

'But did he have any message for you? Say, any suggestions on how to market the antiques yourself?'

Lovejoy sighed. 'I'm afraid not. As you might gather from my deserted shop, my new retirement enterprise has had a sticky start. Even my first customer of the morning wasn't here to buy; he simply had a complaint about what he said I'd sold him.'

Irene glanced around. Then she spotted the golden clock, still ticking away on the counter. 'Was this the item he was complaining about?'

Lovejoy blinked. 'Gracious me, Irene, you're very perceptive. Yes, it was.'

'And what was his complaint?'

'He said it had started to run slow. More or less bamboo-zled me into having a look at it for him. In the end I persuaded him to leave it with me for a couple of days.' He shrugged. 'I've no idea what I'll do with it now he's gone.'

'I've come across a few mis-behaving clocks in my time,' said Irene. 'D'you want me to have a look?'

'Oh, please.'

She reached across the counter and seized the timepiece. Carefully she lifted it up and then peered underneath. 'I'd say this might be the problem.'

She reached in and pulled out a small black plastic box. It must have been held in by the attraction of a strong magnet, for it was hard to remove. She plonked it in front of him.

'Any idea what this is, Lovejoy?'

He shook his head. 'I'm sorry, Irene, I haven't a clue.'

'I'd say it's a GPS tracker. Sends off its location every time it's moved. Rich folk stick them under their Mercedes. That's to locate them, of course, in case they are stolen.'

Lovejoy could hardly believe it. 'And someone's fixed one under this clock? Incredible. Anyway, why should it make the thing go slow?'

'A strong magnet can slightly distort a metal spring. Enough to make it slow down a little. It'll probably be fine now.'

There was a pause while Lovejoy took stock, realising how much he had to learn. He was a complete novice compared with his visitor.

'It was a miracle you found it, Irene.'

She smiled. 'Well, I knew there was one in here some-where.'

Lovejoy blinked. Had he heard aright? 'What?'

Irene paused to put her thoughts in order. 'I've been monitoring the signal for days. I just wasn't sure which object it was now hidden in.'

The dealer's mouth dropped open. 'I don't understand.'

'Well, until this morning, Lovejoy, the GPS trace was somewhere in Waddesdon Manor. Then it came here. But there are only a few objects it could be hidden in. Pictures are too flat, for example, and most ornaments are too slim. The clock was by far the most likely. Especially once you'd told me its provenance.'

Lovejoy's brain was hurting as he tried to hold the ideas together.

'So you were the one to install the tracker inside this clock in the first place?' Then a further thought struck him. 'You must have known my predecessor? Was he the person you were hoping to see?'

Irene shook her head. 'Oh no. I knew he'd gone. He got out just in time, I reckon. The police were onto him.'

This was starting to sound like a script for a black comedy. 'No doubt helped by your tracker, hidden in one of his antiques?'

Irene smiled. 'Renaming the location certainly helped.'

There was a further pause as Lovejoy struggled to take it all in.

'But even if he'd sold the clock, and you could track where it had gone, why should that concern the police?'

'It wouldn't bother them at all, provided the clock just made one journey. But I tracked it to the Manor, then to somewhere else, then back here again. A full circuit. Which was repeated three times in two years.'

Lovejoy's face shifted from deeply puzzled to completely bewildered. 'I'm sorry, Irene. I still don't quite see . . .'

'It was a massive insurance scam, Lovejoy. The purchaser

bought the clock and made sure it was heavily insured. Then it was stolen. The purchaser claimed the insurance. Meanwhile, a while later, the thieves came here and sold it back to your predecessor.'

Light was starting to dawn. But as it did Lovejoy could see a snag. 'But surely, that would only work once?'

'It would if there was only one antiques insurance company,' said Irene. 'But there are plenty out there. The clock was bought again; the owner repeated the process with different insurers, netting more "compensation". It was when he did the same thing for the third time that I decided to act. That was when the police got involved.'

Lovejoy mused for a moment and then nodded. 'I see. I assume you work for one of these companies?'

'Well, I did.'

Once more he was surprised. 'But top management must have been delighted. Tracking locations on key antiques is revolutionary. The technology's only been possible for the last few years. It gives a silver lining to a dark black cloud. Surely, you'd earned promotion?'

'You might think so, Lovejoy. But insurance companies are male strongholds. At least mine was. The directors couldn't bring themselves to concede that a woman had thought of the idea.' She grimaced, 'I didn't crash through the plate-glass ceiling. I bounced off it and landed back on the floor, battered and bruised.'

'Irene, that's awful.' There was a pause and then another question occurred to him. 'But you are still employed?'

'I'm still in insurance. But these days I'm operating below the radar. You see, no-one else bothers with tracking antiques. But it leads me to rich homes with guilty secrets. Who are happy to pay to keep things that way. In fact, I gather far more nowadays than I would ever have done in insurance.'

There was a pause. Then she saw his face light up as the penny finally dropped.

Irene posed the key question. 'Maybe, Lovejoy, you'd let me put a few more trackers round in your antiques?'

14 THE MASTER'S LAST STAND

'It's a sticky day, Victor,' remarked his fellow commentator.

'Especially for Geoffrey.'

It was the last match of the summer. The crowd was sizeable. The main attraction was to see the man they called "Master", who'd recently hinted at retirement.

Victor sighed. 'Trouble is, we're meant to sound exciting. That's what our listeners expect. Spoilt by one-day cricket. But it's nothing like what he delivers.'

'Never has been,' said the colleague. 'Security's his strong suit. Could do with a bit more of it in the Test side.'

There was a pause. Then there was action on the field and Victor leant forward into his microphone. 'And now the two Captains are on the field. . . the coin's been flipped. . . he's lost.'

'He'll still be their hero. He reached his ceiling – captained England and Yorkshire.'

'Though he was sacked both times,' recalled Victor. 'Once on the day the second Pope of the year died.'

'Right. You mean the poor bloke's been starved of publicity?'

'Hardly. The Yorkshire Post headline that day was: "Boycott sacked as Yorkshire Captain". And in tiny letters at the foot of the page: "Pope's death shocks the world".'

The Visitors batted first. They weren't "England" but had plenty who still hoped for the honour.

Fifty overs were sufficient for a good batsman to make his mark. The score mounted steadily. By the end they'd reached 250.

Lunch was taken before the home side responded. The Master himself was down to open.

'How was Geoff's side chosen?' asked Victor, glancing down the scorecard. 'It looks a motley crew.'

'His own choice. Players that he'd forgotten he'd fallen out with; or ones he owed a favour, from having run them out too often.'

'Local?'

'They all live this end of Yorkshire. He didn't want high travel expenses.'

Victor shook his head. The umpires emerged and the afternoon began.

In his prime the Master had faced, and often conquered, the fiercest bowlers in the world. He averaged over fifty. Twice he'd managed to average a hundred over a whole season.

'Attacking strokes spring out of an immaculate defence,' opined Victor. 'These days they're few and far between – but his defence is still solid.'

Nevertheless, the commentators' object was to make the event sound exciting.

Victor mused on. 'When you get old, the last things you forget are the things you learned first. Geoff's long forgotten how to attack but he can still remember how to defend. It'll be up to his team to get the runs – if they get 'em at all.'

At first the crowd purred contentedly, watching their hero pottering around, scoring occasionally. Successive batting partners grappled with alternate overs of pace and spin.

Most made twenty or thirty and then got out. But the team

were falling behind; and the spectators, who'd come expecting a win, began to murmur.

Many had begun their drinking in late morning. Now they started to get restless.

Suddenly there was commotion in the stand. To loud cheers, a pretty, red-haired female started stripping off. Once completely naked, she clambered over the boundary board and onto the field of play.

'Here's something for you, Victor. A streaker. You'd better describe this, it's more your expertise than mine.'

Victor grimaced at the hospital-pass handover but then warmed to the task.

'The game's half sleep, this might wake it up. A female, highly agile. Half the age of most of the players.' He laughed. 'Removing her might prove something of a challenge.'

A pause, then: 'She's on the pitch now. Wants to give them a chance, I suppose. I'm not sure Geoffrey approves.'

For the local hero had moved away from the crease and was eying the intruder warily.

The streaker ran towards his stumps, skipped and leap-frogged over. But still she wasn't apprehended.

'They've not got enough stewards out there, Victor.'

'Maybe they cost too much?'

Now, more daring, the woman was performing cartwheels in mid pitch. After which she headed for the stumps at the captain's end.

But the local hero had had enough. As she jumped the stumps again, he swung his bat and caught her bottom. There was an audible thump and she tripped over. A moment later she was seized by the wicketkeeper and handed over to the police.

Victor was a happy man. 'I'd say that's Geoffrey's best shot so far.'

His colleague focussed his binoculars. 'Duncan Fearnley's bat-maker's symbol is smudged on her. She'll remember the day, anyway. Maybe it'll refocus Geoffrey's energies.'

By late afternoon the home side were on 180 for 7, with the Master a modest but respectable 43. There were 6 overs left and 70 runs needed. They'd need to score an unlikely twelve runs an over to beat the Visitors.

'I'm afraid the home side's not going to win this,' observed Victor. He was paid to be impartial, but he had a soft spot for Geoffrey, whom he'd watched through childhood. He had an early memory of the Master on television, scoring his first century against the Australians; and he'd kept watching ever since.

The crowd didn't think much of the home side's chances either and started to get restive. An informal conga formed at the back of the stand. It jostled and shuffled down to the front, blocking the view for seated spectators.

At first the dance looked harmless; but its length grew. Even an old man – or someone dressed up as an old man – joined in, waving his walking stick.

Collective memories of the streaker took hold. If she could invade the pitch and hold up play for ten minutes, why shouldn't they? Wouldn't it be better for the game to be abandoned than to end in a humiliating defeat?

So without much ado, the conga headed out onto the pitch. There was no chance of them outrunning the players. But they did outnumber them by a factor of twenty. The stewards in the stands seemed reluctant to move onto the field. For a few minutes there was total mayhem.

The crowd were not hostile to the cricketers. Many wanted

to shake the hand of their hero on the cricket field. Geoffrey was surrounded by vigorous and well-inebriated admirers; but he seemed to appreciate their attentions.

But even the best of times come to an end. The arrival of a policeman was enough to cajole the spectators back to their stand.

The game could resume. The last act was about to be played.

Only when Geoffrey took guard for the next ball was it realised that he had lost his bat. He'd laid it down to hug his admirers and it was no longer behind him. Someone in the crowd had managed to exchange it for the walking stick.

But the Master didn't seem to mind, maybe still in his own heaven from the welcome he'd just received.

'Geoffrey always claimed he could bat with a stick of rhubarb,' recalled Victor. 'This is his chance to demonstrate.'

Fortunately the bowler he was facing was a slow leg-spinner – the kind England hadn't perfected for half a century. Shane Warne he was not. He walked back a few paces then trundled up to the crease.

The Master hadn't faced as gentle a ball as this for several decades. Even he couldn't bring himself to play it defensively. He took a stride forward and waited for it to arrive. Then swung his walking stick with such exquisite timing that the ball disappeared off the field and into the stand. The sequence was greeted with amazed applause.

That was the first ball of the over; and the bowler's first of the match. It did nothing to boost his confidence. The next ball was a little faster but misdirected. Once more the Master waited and then hit it out of the ground. It completed his half century and caused rapturous applause.

The umpire declared the next one was a "no-ball". But by now the Master didn't care. It was within his reach; and so also heaved into the stand.

The next ball was accurate but slow. He had no need even to stretch. Six more runs followed.

By now the bowler was a nervous wreck. He still needed three more deliveries to complete the over and he'd completely lost his rhythm.

Eighteen runs later, with the Master now on 85 and his team's score 222, the over was finally over.

In desperation the visiting captain recalled his star fast bowler. But the Master was no longer on strike. Instead was a young allrounder with a glittering future, who liked fast bowling immensely.

Six balls later, each one caressed for four, the locals had reached 246 and needed just five more runs to win. And the Master was on strike once more.

The visiting captain did have other options. But this wasn't the moment. Instead he tossed the ball to the leg spinner: 'One last try?'

Which proved as hopeless as before.

The Master took one big stride and clobbered it into the stand: against all the odds, his team had won.

Later, in the dressing room, Geoffrey spoke to his team.

'As you know, lads, I've always loved batting. But last week I saw the specialist. I've been diagnosed with throat cancer: they're operating on me next week. None of us can keep going for ever. All we can ever do is to try our very best. If you never see me again, lads, try and remember that.'

15   BREAK A LEG

On Monday evenings Miles Henderson would go on what he called a "marketing campaign" to the pub-quiz at the Grindstone, while Sally stayed comfortably at home. She was glad of any wins in these dark, recessionary times.

But when Miles returned, announcing he'd just won a contract to redecorate the local theatre – 'from their new livewire director' – Sally Henderson didn't realise quite what she was in for. She'd always had an interest in the theatre, though she'd hoped when young to be on the stage, rather than merely to paint one.

It was only when they stood inside the auditorium, preparing to start the work, that she thought seriously about the height of the premises; and realised that, as the supposedly feisty partner, she would be the one up high, wielding her paintbrush.

It was a long way down.

'I don't think we've a ladder that goes that high,' she murmured, trying to suppress her fears. It wasn't often she lacked confidence.

But Miles was ahead of her. 'It's alright, I checked. The theatre's got a tower platform that will reach the ceiling. They use it to focus the lighting, and to replace the occasional bulb.'

Sally wasn't altogether convinced but could only pin her hopes on Miles' advanced planning. It was usually reliable.

'Yet another contract to be completed against the clock,' she remarked. For it turned out the winter pantomime was due to open at the theatre in just six weeks.

'It's tight but do-able,' declared Miles, the optimist.

What Miles hadn't been told by the slippery director was that the theatre would be occupied for several weeks beforehand for rehearsals. They only had a couple of weeks on their own before every action needed coordinating with the "Thespians".

The Hendersons were used to time-pressure, working long into the evening when required. They managed to blitz some of the work – the dressing rooms and the ticket office – while the place was empty. And when the actors did appear, they proved extremely friendly.

The director, Damian, claimed he'd been "brought in to instil professional standards". Miles murmured to Sally that might make him harder to get alongside.

The pantomime was a version of "Jack and the Giant Beanstalk", expanded for a modern audience. One new feature involved an actor seated on a narrow chair, fastened by a rope to the auditorium roof. At the vital moment in the production she was to swing out over the audience, dropping bunches of flowers on receptive-looking females.

To Sally it looked scary: the actress playing the flower girl, Carys, didn't look over-confident either. There was no safety belt; she had to hold on with one hand while showering flowers with the other. But Damian gave her no choice. 'The key to targeting, my dear, is to choose where on the stage you take off from.' He insisted on her trying it again and again, till she could reach every corner of the auditorium.

By now Miles had accessed the theatre's high tower. They tried it after rehearsals. It wasn't easy to move; because of auditorium seating the legs always had to be arranged straddling a row of seats.

'We'll need to paint as much we can from one location, then go onto the next,' Miles observed.

Sally noted the royal "we". She climbed the tower gingerly. It wobbled more than she'd expected and took her some time to reach the swinging platform on the top.

But at least it had a handrail. She could reach a long way as the platform was swung around. As long as she didn't look down, she told herself, she'd be fine.

'We'd better not try to move it while they're rehearsing,' warned Sally. 'It creaks like mad. Damian might not approve.'

'OK. We'll shift it in the evenings,' Miles replied. 'Ten different bases should be enough to reach the whole ceiling. If we work weekends, we can just do it in time.'

For several weeks all went smoothly. The actors got the hang of the plot (such as it was) while the Hendersons progressed steadily with their painting. Sally was mostly up high while Miles did the fiddly painting down below.

But the opening night drew steadily closer. Finally they reached the morning of the dress rehearsal.

And then came the calamity.

It was a much-disrupted rehearsal. Damian still had plenty to say. They'd reached the scene where Carys "flew" over the audience. By now she was oozing confidence.

But this time a jazz band was playing. Carys misheard Damian's instructions, headed to audience right rather than stage right. Where she crashed into the tower, just below where Sally was busy painting.

The tower wobbled scarily but was well-secured and stayed vertical. Carys would have been alright, too, if she had held on.

But for some reason she let go of the rope. Then she lost her balance, fell off and crashed down onto the seats below. She broke her left leg in two places in the process.

The dress rehearsal came to an abrupt standstill as the girl howled in agony.

Traffic was heavy and the ambulance took a while getting to the theatre. Then the crew had to clamber around the tower. A few minutes later the luckless Carys was being rushed to hospital.

Back in the theatre, the recriminations began.

Damian tried to put the blame on to Carys. 'She should have hung on tighter,' he declared.

But the shocked actors were all on her side and refused to accept that. And made it clear that none of them was willing to act as a replacement flower girl.

Rebuffed, Damian turned to the decorators. But Miles was quick to point out that the tower carried the correct warning signs; and hadn't been moved during today's rehearsal. He also pointed out that he and Sally were working to a tight contract; this was their final day.

As opinions were exchanged and tempers rose, someone suggested they all take a break.

Sally decided someone ought to go and visit Carys and it might as well be her.

By the time Sally had reached the hospital, Carys had passed through A&E and reached the acute ward. She still had on her flower-girl outfit but was now draped with medical apparatus; her left leg was in a massive plaster. She was conscious though in a lot of pain. But put on a brave smile when she saw Sally.

'Carys, you poor girl, we're all so sorry. Can you remember

what happened?'

Carys grimaced. 'I hadn't expected to see that bloody tower right in front of me. Then something sticky landed on my hand – the one that was holding the rope. Instinctively I let go. Then I toppled. And now I'm here.'

Sally didn't pursue the question of what the sticky item might have been. But she had been painting directly above the girl before the fall; and felt terribly guilty.

Once the company had regrouped after their coffee break, more immediate aspects came into focus. The opening night was imminent.

'The question right now,' said the director, 'is, who is going to replace her?'

'Why replace her at all?' asked the leading lady. 'The flower girl's hardly vital to the plot.'

Many supported her. But Damian was attached to the flying florist concept. Miles recalled it was in the pantomime's local advertising. Presumably the pictures had come from when he'd used the idea elsewhere.

The issue was still being fiercely debated when Sally rejoined them.

'Look, I'll give it a go if you're that desperate,' she offered. 'I'm used to heights, anyway.'

Damian looked overwhelmed. 'Sally, that would be wonderful. We'd better get started on your outfit.'

'I'd rather start rehearsing the flights. And if you are fitting me with a new outfit, I've an idea for a safety belt.'

Sally was hastily trained, ready for the opening night. Her opening performance was uneven, but the audience didn't care: the rest of the production had plenty of rough edges too.

But the reviews next day were better than adequate.

Miles monitored from behind the stage, there for his wife if anything went wrong.

The nights went by and performances improved – even for Sally. Every night Miles would take her home and lavish her with praise.

Then, one evening, he noticed someone he knew in the audience. He puzzled for a while, then remembered: he'd been a mate of Damian in the pub-quiz where this had all started.

Miles didn't think anything of it. Then he noticed him again the next night; and the one after. Was he a pantomime junkie? Though he was pleased to see that the man was sitting well away from Sally's flight path.

The same thing happened night after night. It was too often to be coincidence. Now Miles stopped watching his wife's flight and focused his attention on the man.

Next night Miles brought his binoculars for a closer look and was even more alarmed. He took a picture of the persistent pantomimer. Then he went to see the police.

Next day he had a companion watcher. The day after that there was a minor commotion. The man was arrested as the flower girl soared.

'So what was all that about?' asked Sally, as they wandered home.

'The bloke used the targeted distraction of your flights to pickpocket his neighbours. I spotted him doing it every night. Tonight the police caught him red-handed.'

'But I only flew where Damian told me,' Sally protested. 'He must have been part of the scam as well.'

'Trouble is, Sally, that's much harder to prove. Damian's a

slippery fish. I wonder where he'll be moving on to?'

'Oh, Carys told me,' she replied. 'His next production, she said, was going to be Oliver Twist. I wonder who he'll have as his next Fagan?'

16   OLD PECULIAR

I can't tell you how, but somehow I'd managed to find time for amateur dramatics, in the midst of my full-time job as a police officer. Maybe it helped that I was black; and the play itself was a study in unintended racism.

I didn't tell my colleagues about it, there was enough incipient racism at the police station already. That's apart from my friend Inspector Jim Salting, of course. He was an outsider like me: he'd been unlucky enough to work in the Met before emigrating to Scarborough.

The play was entitled "Old Peculiar" and set in a run-down pub. The main character was a gruff Yorkshire landlord called Sam, who'd just taken on a West Indian barmaid – that was played by me, Lauren Shaw. The appointment aroused fierce criticism from most of the customers, who were all "chalk white and proud of it". The play explored how their reactions evolved and were partially resolved – after a fashion. But also the effect on the landlord, whom I'm afraid the play saw being driven to deep despair.

Like the centre peg in a croquet lawn, I was bang in the middle as the various battles raged. I didn't speak many lines; the main challenge was ignoring the insults from one clique or another. Of course, these were only lines penned by the playwright: I'd heard worse in the police station. I pretended not to take it to heart. But I can tell you, it wasn't easy.

We had rehearsed in a local church hall and were to perform

there over the weekend. The backstage staff had prepared the set on stage: it was simple, a few tables and chairs, set around a working bar.

This was our first performance. We were new kids on the block. No-one knew what sort of audience we would get, or how many. We'd set out thirty seats in the hall, but we had more at the back if required. We were a bunch of amateurs, we each had a practical job as well as performing: mine was selling tickets at the door. A time for my most smiley face to hide my first-night nerves.

The customers were mostly white but friendly enough. I judged that the takings, over the three planned performances, should cover production costs such as the hire of the hall. There wouldn't be enough left to support any local charity. Not this year, anyway.

The audience were mostly local, couples or pairs of female friends. One exception was an intense woman with a frown, dark-framed glasses and a notebook. I assumed she would be reporting on the event for the Scarborough Echo – I could be famous at last!

There was also my mum, who'd come over specially from Bradford. It was good to know I'd have one solid supporter.

I heard the bell behind the stage go 'ding' and slipped away to change into my barmaid outfit, more daring than my normal attire. I'd last worn a blouse as sheer as this when I was a teenager. Mind, it was rather offset by my overdone makeup.

Ready at last. The curtains parted, a full house was revealed, and the play began.

As a first night it started pretty well. Sam was an experienced actor and quickly won over the audience as the Old Peculiar landlord, with his broad accent and caustic asides. He explained his last-chance scheme: to win extra customers by taking on a fetching new assistant.

My consequential stage interview for the post of barmaid went better than I'd dared to hope. I was well into the production by now. I wasn't Lauren the off-duty policewoman; I was Molly the Dolly, poised to greet customers and rebut prejudice with charm and a smile.

The next scene saw tensions start to build as Old Peculiar customers came in and saw who was serving. Initial reactions were muted but weren't masked for long. Comments started to fly; and the factions formed. And so, scene by scene and row by row, the play continued. It almost became violent. At one point I had to intervene to separate two groups that were heading for a punch-up and got a pint of bitter thrown over me. It was that sort of a pub.

By the end Sam was in despair. It was clear his last throw of the dice hadn't worked. Standing beside him, I watched in simulated horror as he opened one of the drawers behind the bar. Then he pulled out a revolver and pointed it towards himself.

It was my chance to be the play's heroine. I threw myself on to him, trying to avoid disaster. But it was too late. The gun went off close by my ear as Sam slumped to the floor.

In the ensuing silence the stage curtains were swiftly closed.

What should have happened next – what we'd rehearsed – was that Sam would stand up, the cast would assemble in a line, the curtains would re-open and we would all take a final bow. Leaving the audience to imagine what might happen next as they wandered home.

But it didn't happen this way tonight. For the noise of the gun was far louder than I'd heard in rehearsal, when it had been loaded with blanks.

And this time Sam wasn't moving at all.

I disentangled myself as fast as I could from the fallen body, no longer a bohemian barmaid with excess makeup but a police officer reacting to an emergency.

'Ring 999,' I ordered. 'Get an ambulance. That was a real bullet.'

I saw the Director give a concerned nod and pull out his phone.

'And we'd better call the police,' I went on. 'Shouldn't we send the audience home? That'd keep whatever's happened private for a little longer.'

The Director took my point and slipped out between the curtains to address the audience. 'There's been a minor incident. An ambulance is on its way. It would be really helpful to us if you all made you ways home as quietly as possible. Thank you so much for your support. We'll put out a press release as soon as we have any news.'

Backstage, the rest of the cast were silent, numb with shock. I knelt down beside Sam, still comatose on the stage floor. I felt his wrist – there was a faint heartbeat. And I checked: he was still breathing.

'Sam's still alive,' I reported to the company, 'but we mustn't move him. The ambulance crew will do that.'

Ten minutes went by. The audience complied with the Director's plea and slipped out. Then the ambulance crew arrived and took over.

Soon a stretcher was produced and Sam was hustled off to the hospital.

Five minutes later the police appeared.

I'd been hoping they'd send Jim. I was upset and shaken by

what had happened, needed a friend to talk to. But it wasn't Jim.

Worse still, the two officers who came didn't recognise me in my costume and makeup. I recognised them, though: privately I thought of them as Wallace and Gromit. They were a major part of the police station's loutish tendency.

The Director outlined what had happened.

'In the final scene, Sam was supposed to commit suicide. There was a gun in the drawer here and he took it out. The barmaid here, Molly, tried to stop him, threw herself onto him, but the gun went off in the struggle. Somehow, tonight, the blank was a real bullet and Sam was hit. He's now in intensive care.'

'So where's the gun?' asked Wallace. It was the obvious question.

Gromit slipped on some plastic gloves. Then he crouched down, peered under the bar and pulled out an old-fashioned revolver.

'Was this the gun?' he asked. The Director glanced briefly and nodded.

'Who loaded it?'

I knew this was the key question. I held my breath.

'It was me,' the stage manager responded. 'Ten minutes before the play started. But I swear, all the bullets I put in were blanks. I don't have anything else.'

Wallace mused for a moment, staring at the set and the cast. 'So who was behind the bar during the performance?'

'Just the landlord and the barmaid,' replied the Director. 'The rest were all pub customers, sat at those tables on the other side.'

'Right,' said the officer. 'In that case we'd better take Molly here down to the station for further questioning.'

My mouth dropped open. I certainly hadn't seen this coming.

You might be wondering why I didn't just tell the officers that I was a police officer like them. If there had been a crime, I was surely worth talking to: I had the inside track as a key witness.

The trouble was, I'd heard nasty rumours in the police station about how these two treated witnesses, especially young women. Being a female police officer, especially one who was black, might only make this worse. So I decided, for better or worse, to remain silent.

I was given no chance to collect my coat but marched straight out to the police car. Ten minutes later we reached the station. I was taken down to a basement interview room and left to wait.

I sat there for half an hour. There was no heating and my see-through blouse didn't do much to keep me warm. What on earth were my captors doing?

Finally the door opened. Wallace and Gromit appeared and sat down facing me. I could see they'd planned something: there was an evil smile on their faces.

'Molly, you were the only one who could have got at that drawer during the performance. We need to search you, see what else you're carrying.'

'I'm not carrying anything,' I protested.

'Don't worry, we're going to give you a chance to prove it. Just take off every item of your clothing and place them on the table.'

I couldn't believe what I'd just heard. 'If I'm going to be strip-searched, it needs to be done by a female officer.'

Wallace chuckled. 'Sorry, Molly, there are no females on

duty right now. Come on, the sooner you strip the quicker my colleague here can check it all over.'

This was terrible. But what could I do? Right now I could see no choice.

They stood me against the wall and watched with smirking smiles. I reminded myself that I had come here as an actor and I had to perform. I did my best to undress in a non-arousing manner, telling myself that I was getting ready for bed in my flat.

Once I was stark naked, Wallace kept me standing beside the wall while Gromit slowly examined every item I'd removed. By now I was shivering with cold. Of course, they didn't find anything. There was nothing to find.

'See,' I said. 'I told you there was nothing. Can I get dressed again, please? I'm very cold.' This was the acid test: was my ordeal over or had they more to add?

Thankfully, I never found out. For at that moment I heard a voice I recognised outside the door.

'Open up, please. This is Inspector Salting.'

Wallace looked as guilty as hell. But it was the voice of authority and he had to comply. Gromit didn't even have time to hide my clothes before Jim appeared with a face like thunder.

He took in the scene in an instant. 'Give the lady back her clothes. The superintendent will be wanting to see you two first thing tomorrow morning. And then get out of my sight.'

Hastily, I grabbed my barmaid clothes and put them back on as Wallace and Gromit disappeared like rats fleeing a trap.

Five minutes later Jim escorted me back upstairs. He looked furious but didn't speak until we were out of the station. 'My car's round the back. We'll get back to the church hall and pick up your coat. Then, if you're up for it, I'd like to take you out for supper.'

I was still taking in my rescue, a host of questions crowded into my mind. But one was uppermost.

'Is there any news on Sam?'

'He's still in intensive care, Lauren, but don't worry. The doctors are confident he'll pull through.'

I almost cried in relief. The storm clouds had at least one silver lining.

It wasn't that late; the cast were still in the church hall, trying to make sense of it all. As was my Mum: I realised now how Jim had come to be involved. The Scarborough Echo reporter was lurking there as well.

I was hungry but couldn't just walk out, too much had gone on. I clapped my hands, 'Guys, could we all sit down, please. Try and work out what really happened.'

I sensed this was what the others were wanting too. As I got onto my stool behind the bar, I noticed something I'd not seen before, which put a fresh idea in my mind.

'I've a question for the stage manager,' I began. 'Could you tell us, Billy, how we got this furniture? It's highly realistic.'

It was better than being asked about blank bullets, anyway. Billy smiled. 'There was an old pub on the far side of Scarborough, the Last Chance, that was closing down. The landlord had committed suicide, the regular drinkers had moved on and the administrators were glad to get rid of everything. I hired a van, the Director and I went over and brought back the lot. No wonder it's realistic.'

It was an answer I could work with. 'Billy, did you check for yourself that all the cupboards and drawers were empty?'

'It was being given away, Lauren. I just assumed they would be.'

111

Jim, at least, sensed where I was heading and gave me an encouraging smile. But he didn't intervene: recognised that this was my case.

'The thing is,' I continued, 'Sam always took the weapon you'd prepared out of the drawer on the left. But tonight – I only thought about it afterwards – he opened the one on the right. So the intended weapon – the one he'd rehearsed with – might still be in the left-hand drawer. Could we see?'

There was silence as the Director stepped forward and opened the drawer. 'You're right, Lauren. It's still there.'

'Don't touch it,' warned Jim. 'We need to check for Billy's fingerprints.'

'So,' I concluded, 'Sam didn't pick up the gun he was expecting. The one he seized tonight had been in there for ages. It's likely the Last Chance landlord had inserted the live ammunition himself. So tonight, I'm afraid to say, has all been just a dreadful accident.'

I glanced round: the rest of the cast were looking highly relieved.

The reporter, though, had just disappeared. Maybe I'd see a pale silver lining of my own when her article appeared?

17   DOUBLE JEOPARDY

Despite reaching the ripe old age of sixty-five, Billy Henderson was still on the books of the Yorkshire Guards. He performed ceremonial duties, providing protection where there was no real risk. It wasn't clear, as his son Miles observed to his wife Sally, why he hadn't been pensioned off years ago.

The sad truth was that Billy had nowhere else to go. His partner was long dead, his only other relatives were in Australia. His health was too worrisome for him to join them – the price of decades of smoking. The younger Hendersons were far too busy with their thriving decorating business to give him much time and Sally found him hard to get on with anyway. Only politeness forced a minimal contact to be maintained.

Billy Henderson's most notable feature was his outsized ears, which he claimed 'made him look like King Charles'. He took pleasure in the minutiae of ritual, which drove the effervescent Sally crackers.

The relationship, such as it was, continued for years, until Billy finally announced he was "being retired".

'Before I stop, let me show you both round where I work.' In the circumstances they could scarcely decline.

They met at the Town Hall. Billy led them into the main auditorium and pointed to the stage at the far end. 'If my double, Charles, dies in Yorkshire, this'll be where they'll rest his coffin, on its way to London. It's been my job to guard it.' He sounded immensely proud.

'On your own?' asked Sally, trying desperately not to sound sceptical.

'Oh no. That camera behind us is focused on the stage. If there's trouble the Guards will send reinforcements fast enough. I just stand at attention beside it whenever I'm on duty.'

Sally was tempted to argue further but saw Miles shaking his head. His dad might as well be doing something he loved. There was no point in upsetting him.

A week later King Charles was taken ill while out shooting on the North York Moors. Buckingham Palace gave few details, except to say he was being treated in a Lodge on the Bransdale Estate.

Most of the nation weren't that bothered. Charles hadn't yet made himself a hero. In the North of England he vied for unpopularity with the latest Prime Minister. There was speculation in the Yorkshire Post as to who was disliked the most.

But his illness made Sally Henderson think of her father-in-law; and feel guilty about how little time they had given him. She urged Miles to phone the Barracks.

'Odd,' he reported back. 'He's not there. They gave him a send-off yesterday, haven't seen him since.'

Concern hit Sally. 'Miles, surely, when he was finally leaving, he'd have contacted us? Unless . . . he was taken ill or something.'

'We can't do anything right now, love. We've only got one day left to complete our latest contract. If we haven't heard anything by tomorrow, I promise we'll go down to the Barracks and make enquiries of our own.'

When they eventually fought their way inside past endless security, they sensed the Barracks weren't exactly pleased to see them. 'Billy was sad to leave the Guards,' the commanding officer said. 'Quite maudlin. He insisted on performing his last afternoon of duty in the Town Hall. We haven't seen him since. Mind, we've been busy ourselves with this scare over King Charles.'

Meanwhile, in the further reaches of Bransdale, one or two obscure reporters, sensing a remote chance to make their names, were entrenched outside the Lodge gates. Nicholas Witchell and his ilk were not among them.

They were amazed when a hearse drew up containing an unadorned oak coffin, followed by a military land rover. The driver of the hearse, a man also in uniform, spoke with gate security; then the convoy passed inside.

It was puzzling. Questions started to be asked. Was this simply the best that Bransdale could offer by way of local entertainment? Did the crew they'd seen also sing and dance? Or was Charles a lot more ill than had been admitted?

King Charles' visit to the estate had been a private affair to catch up with an old friend. There were no garden parties to open or attend. Queen Camilla was dining in luxury in Windsor Castle; here Charles was making do with local staff. It was rumoured he'd declared it 'amounted almost to camping'.

The hearse drove slowly up the drive to the Lodge and round to the stables at the rear, followed by the land rover. Six soldiers disembarked and stood to attention.

Smartly, sombrely, they marched up to the hearse. Then, in a manoeuvre they'd obviously practised elsewhere, they withdrew the coffin and carried it inside the Lodge. Finally, they laid it down to rest, on a large bench in the lower chamber.

It was the chef who noticed first. She had to pass through the chamber to reach the vegetable store beyond – King Charles might think Bransdale was 'little better than camping', but he still expected top notch meals.

There was a noise coming from the coffin.

The chef was not a woman of notable imagination. She'd come here for the weekend from the best hotel in Helmsley. Her skills were culinary not forensic. But there was something. Slowly, she circled the coffin table: yes, it definitely came from here.

No more than a faint scratching. Might just be a mouse. But whatever was that doing inside a brand-new coffin?

None of her business, she decided. Maybe it was another Royal fetish? She hastened on to fetch her aubergines and celeriac.

But she couldn't help mentioning it, once back in the kitchen.

Perturbed, another visitor came down to the chamber. This time the Lodge butler.

He didn't generally take much notice of chatter, but this chef wasn't one to make things up. He listened carefully; he too could hear a noise.

But this wasn't just a scratching. There was also a moan. Almost a human moan.

Butlers are the most versatile of staff: they have to cope, unflappably, with all sorts of events. But they like to know exactly what they are dealing with.

A few minutes later the butler had returned, clutching a large screwdriver. And started to unscrew the coffin lid.

In a different world Sally might also have been a butler. She wasn't easy to shake off. The commanding officer soon found he'd more than met his match.

'So the last time anyone saw Billy was when he went on duty two days ago? In full uniform?'

'Of course, madam. We are His Majesty's Guards.'

'On his own?'

'There was nothing there but a large empty coffin. Be different if the King was inside and crowd were filing by to pay their respects.'

Silence. Then Miles recalled Billy had spoken of CCTV. 'Was this being filmed?'

Reluctantly, the commander nodded. 'But it's a special camera. It doesn't record anything when there's no movement. So you won't get four hours of your dad at attention.'

'But can we at least see it?' persisted Sally. 'After all, it is Billy's final performance.'

The commander was under strict orders to refuse such a request: this was a security device, and these were civilians.

But one of the two was Sally, with an irresistible stare.

He sighed. 'OK. I'll let you watch it – but only the once.'

Carefully, reverently, the butler pulled up the coffin lid.

He had been schooled to expect the unexpected. But even he was shocked.

For there was a body inside, in full military uniform. He saw protruding ears. It was . . . it must be the King.

In humble obeisance he fell to his knees, his eyes filled with tears.

All the staff had been told "the King was ill". But something must have happened while he was off-site this afternoon. Quite a lot, if he was now lying in a lead-lined coffin.

He had to get himself up to date, turned and headed for the door. That doctor was due a piece of his mind.

Sally and Miles were shown to a viewing room and Friday's video was selected.

There was something to watch at the start: Billy Henderson, in resplendent uniform, came and stood to attention, facing the empty coffin.

The same image continued, frozen, with a tiny digital clock in the corner.

Then came movement. For it looked as though Billy had fainted. He collapsed forward, straight into the coffin. A few seconds later the lid wobbled, then came slowly down on top of him.

The remainder of the video showed the coffin standing alone. After four hours other soldiers came to screw down the lid and carry it away.

'That was when we heard King Charles was ill,' explained the commander, as shaken as they were. 'We had no idea Billy Henderson was still inside.'

When the butler made his report, the doctor hastened to reassure him that King Charles was still alive. 'He's in his room, updating his diary. Come and see.'

And indeed he was. But the King found the tale intriguing. He joined the others as they headed back to the coffin chamber.

Billy Henderson had just managed to sit himself up inside the open coffin and was peering round, trying to make sense of it all. It didn't look like Sheffield Town Hall.

Then, worst of all, he saw the King appear. Was this a dream? Or a nightmare?

'You know,' said Charles, as he inspected the new arrival, 'we are rather alike. I've always wanted a double, someone

who could be deployed on visits to confuse the press. Especially bloody Witchell.' He smiled at Billy conspiratorially. 'I
don't suppose you'd like the job?'

18   FLIGHT FROM MADNESS

It was back in February that I was dispatched to Europe.

'Sergei,' my boss told me, 'Nord Stream 2, Gazprom's second pipeline to Germany, is now ready to pump; they're negotiating prices. But it's taking for ever: what's really going on?'

I was no KGB agent. I was a mid-rank thinktank analyst. Never been out of Russia in my life. Obviously, I was keen to see the wider world. It sounded right up my street.

I did my homework. The pipelines were controversial. The United States, always hostile to the motherland, was strongly opposed – one of the few policies Trump and Biden agreed on. But Germany – and Western Europe – were strongly in favour. No surprise there – they had almost no gas of their own.

I knew Russia had the world's largest gas reserves. In 2021 half of Europe's gas imports had come from Russia. I was naïve in those days, hoped that in a cooperative world both sides would strive to benefit.

The pipe ended in Germany after winding its way past Denmark, up the Baltic Sea to Narva Bay. The gas started out in Siberia. Operating rules and prices were being thrashed out with the European Union in a Conference Centre in Copenhagen.

I found myself a room nearby, in a small hotel on the quayside. I was amazed at the tariff – how on earth could they claim the West was prosperous? Though I had to admit the sight of the brightly coloured boats chugging up and down was cheerful enough.

The hotel provided breakfast – not the buckwheat porridge I was brought up on, but still quite tasty. I loved those Danish pastries. The meal also brought me into contact with other guests.

I found myself sharing a table with an elegantly dressed, bright-eyed woman called Mathilde. She was also here to follow the pipe-line negotiations. She was Danish but spoke English and Russian; we communicated easily. I gathered she had once worked in Moscow.

Our meeting wasn't such a coincidence: the hotel was round the corner from the Centre. There might be others staying here as well. But Mathilde would do for me.

'The best time to catch up on conference progress,' Mathilde said, 'is over lunch. The less senior delegates eat in the conference restaurant. You and I could slide in and join them.'

Until then she and I explored the quayside. She was keen to enjoy her time in Copenhagen, noting places to dine later. And to be honest, I was enjoying her company.

Lunch was, shall we say, interesting. I was glad I was with Mathilde; she was completely unapologetic about sharing a table with delegates. Nor shy to seek their opinions and reflections. I mostly listened: I sensed support for the Russian viewpoint was limited.

In the afternoon Mathilde and I continued to explore Copenhagen and argue over the pipeline. In the evening we dined together on steak and chips. Hardly surprising, but the wine was better than anything I'd drunk in Moscow.

The pattern continued for the next two weeks. By then I was smitten with Mathilde and I'd claimed her spare bed – the savings on my accommodation covered most of our expenses.

I had only submitted one report (mostly cobbled together from Mathilde's findings) when Ukraine happened.

The Kremlin announced they were "conducting a Special Operation to take over Ukraine. It should take only a few days and lead to closer links between our two countries."

I was told to come home at once. The reason wasn't specified but I feared getting drawn in: I was in my late thirties but had done military service in my youth.

Of course, I talked it over with Mathilde. 'It's a stark choice, Sergei. If you disobey orders, though, you'll never go home again.'

I could see the Operation made Russia very unpopular; it also tainted me. Even so, I was tempted to abscond, but it wasn't clear the Ukraine conflict would last for long. And I'd just bought a small flat in Moscow with my life savings. I couldn't afford to lose it.

When I got back to Moscow I found myself under a cloud; I was cross-examined for days by a government psychologist. I shouldn't have mentioned Mathilde, that made my whole report suspect. I tried to unpack the complexities of economics where some countries were in favour while others were strongly opposed. I championed the pipeline, and how much the gas sales would benefit Russia.

Eventually, grudgingly, my commitment was accepted.

Then the Special Operation went sour. The Ukrainians weren't as pleased to see us as the Kremlin had hoped. The rest of the world were on their side, with talk of 'imposing economic sanctions.'

No-one in Russia took that seriously. Similar threats had

been made after Crimea and nothing came of it. The Europeans would never stay united enough to make it happen.

Months went by. Sanctions bit, costs rose and the situation in Ukraine went from bad to worse. The Ukrainians were tougher than expected and new weapons from the West helped them considerably. It was going to be an uphill struggle.

Then Correction Camps started, for citizens who couldn't understand what the Kremlin was doing. It was a form of Boot Camp, with hard exercise and bland food. I was "volunteered" to visit the nearest one, to lead a weekly discussion on energy economics. Perhaps I had argued too successfully with my psychologist?

No-one in the thinktank really believed talk would change minds. The inmates were hardened opponents, most had been hostile to Putin for years. But now dissent over the Special Operation had given the authorities an excuse to take them off the streets.

My first lecture was a disaster. Attendance was voluntary. All the deep thinkers came along, many looking very rough. No-one cared about a faraway pipeline in a foreign land. Everyone wanted to discuss the evil of invading a neighbouring country.

I had to be very careful: the sessions were monitored on CCTV. I was hardly an enthusiastic warmonger, but I didn't want to go from being a Camp visitor to being a long-term inmate.

I sensed there were a few among my audience who were more open to a wide-ranging discussion. The challenge was to separate them from the hard-liners.

Back at work, I discussed this with other "volunteer" colleagues, who faced similar difficulties. Eventually, a few weeks in, we hit on setting audience homework. We could then have a special feedback session with those that had submitted something, in a later session.

And that was how I encountered Anna.

There weren't many women in the Camp. There were plenty on the streets of Moscow, of course, in the Awkward Squad; but most of these weren't serious threats to stability. Protesting was seen as a fringe activity for the mentally deranged.

Anna had submitted a serious response to my homework. It was one of half a dozen hand-written essays I'd been given to take away and comment on. I was relieved that most of my audience hadn't bothered: it was a manageable workload.

Most entries came from thinking people, glad to argue. Commenting on these was easy.

Anna's essay was different. There were a few pages of economics. Then came something else altogether: a witness statement. It seemed that Anna had been a war reporter in Ukraine and had seen the desolation inflicted by our own troops on the local population.

How should I respond? Was it a trap, to test my loyalty to the establishment? Or a plea for help? I drafted a cautious response, broadly neutral, though I was very disturbed.

The follow-up session was also covered by CCTV, so I had to be careful. I handed back their work and we stuck to economic ideas, with me defending orthodoxy (without much enthusiasm). I didn't say anything outrageous and they accepted that; but I wouldn't stop them expressing their views. My only surprise was that Anna didn't enlarge on her testimony.

The lectures went on; and the discussions. I guessed that Anna was stymied by the camera. She looked to have been badly treated in the recent past; maybe had been threatened with far worse if she spoke about her Ukraine observations to anyone.

Anna had a cheerful, friendly face, not dissimilar to Mathilde. She looked a rarity, an honest journalist. I decided after reflection that this couldn't be a trap. Next time, when she shared more in mid-essay, I responded positively.

I noticed her pleasure as she read my comments, though again no words were spoken. Gradually, week by week, trust between us was established.

Then, one day, her essay contained something brief but far more pressing.

'I have worked out how to escape from the camp. But I need help to get out of the country.'

By now it was September. The war was bogged down and could go on for years. Then came surprising news from Denmark. Leaks had developed in the Gazprom pipelines.

It was a gift to Western propagandists. No-one knew what had really happened, a hundred metres down in the cold Baltic. Which made it easy to ascribe blame. With Russia the easiest target.

My thinktank, a collection of Moscow's leading energy experts, was asked to respond.

As a recent visitor to Denmark, my views were sought. 'We need someone who knows the context,' I said. 'Who can enlarge on the uncertainties – which certainly exist – and who has a slim chance of being believed.'

'That's the problem, Sergei,' they responded. 'What's the solution?'

I drew a breath: was this my chance?

'I met one Danish energy expert who speaks fluent Russian,' I recalled. 'She's an independent thinker. Could we invite her to come here and brief us; perhaps even act as our spokesman?'

The idea was kicked around; no-one had a better suggestion. And the pipeline rumpus was growing.

So I rang my friend Mathilde, and after a preliminary chat invited her to Moscow.

Mathilde responded at once. 'I'm puzzled by the pipeline failures too. I'd be happy to brief your colleagues; and to contribute to a wider debate.'

She arrived via Finland a few days later; and I took her to our visitors' flat. Which was where the idea was sparked.

I was due in the Correction Camp next day. I hastily augmented my comment on Anna's cry for help: 'We could meet in a nearby village.' Then I invited everyone in the feedback seminar to submit ideas for future lectures. That gave Anna a chance to send me a time and date: 'Eleven a.m.; two days' time'. I nodded and gave a tiny smile.

When I left the Camp that day, I had a lot to do.

The first thing was to visit Mathilde. She was still settling in. I outlined the situation regarding Anna and what I needed. To my relief she was eager to help.

Then I went to the railway station; and after that to a charity shop.

Two days later I pleaded a hospital appointment and slipped out of the office mid-morning. Drove to the village I'd specified and waited with bated breath.

Anna's not in full control of her situation, I told myself. *She might be late; or not even turn up at all. She might have been spotted by camp guards and now be subject to brutal interrogation.* But whatever happened, my life was now bound up with hers.

Then I saw a pizza-boy coming down the lane. Or rather, someone dressed in the standard green delivery uniform. I blinked: it was Anna.

I pushed open the passenger door and she slipped in. I let in the clutch and we were off.

There was no time now for idle chatter. 'How long have we got, Anna, before they'll realise you're missing?'

She smiled. 'I complained of feeling very sick – hinted at menstrual problems. That always puts the guards off. We've probably got till this evening.'

'Great. Right now we're heading into Moscow. I have a friend who will help us. Trouble is, she's foreign. Someone might be watching her flat.'

It was a familiar problem in Russia. 'Mm. Could I go in as a pizza boy?'

I shook my head. 'Sorry. That's not credible for a foreign visitor. But look in the back seat. There's a gas-man's jacket and cap. How d'you fancy being a meter reader?'

Silence fell. We were both too tense to talk.

I pulled into a side road and nodded. 'That's my friend's flat. Knock at the door and she'll let you in. Her name's Mathilde. The two of you must swap clothes. Then come back here.'

'What'll happen to Mathilde?'

'She'll wait five minutes till we've gone, then leave, dressed as the meter reader. If anyone is watching, we're all accounted for. Mathilde will take a change of clothes and come back half an hour later. With a bit of luck that'll keep us all off radar.'

Anna nodded, braced herself then headed for the flat. Ten minutes later a chic woman minced daintily down the road. She got in and we headed for the station, parking in long stay.

Lots of cars there; my nondescript Riva would take a while to spot.

'Right,' I said. 'This is Mathilde's ticket, and this is her passport. We're heading for Helsinki. The only train of the day leaves in twenty minutes. Our seats are booked in carriage D.'

Fifteen hours later, our backgrounds exchanged and the border crossed, Anna and I disembarked in Helsinki. I found a way to post Mathilde's passport rapidly back to Moscow. All being well she'd have it back in the next few days. Using it for a repeat journey once she'd finished in Moscow might be tricky, but she was a resourceful woman, up for the challenge.

The immediately challenge for Anna and I was to obtain visas that would allow us to remain in the European Union.

There was a longer-term question we hardly dared ask: would Putin beat a retreat? Or would he move his forces on from Ukraine to the Baltic States? Or even to Finland?

AUTHOR'S REFLECTIONS

I am sometimes asked how my stories arose. This collection has various starting points.

"Flight from Mariupol" was my entry for our Writers' Circle competition in 2022: it had to be about a journey.

In May the Russian invasion of Ukraine was still in its early stages; the news was full of tales of refugees fleeing to Kyiv. So that's where I started. Then I realised that it would make for a more surprising story if the journey was actually across Russia. The hard work arose in thinking of an unexpected ending.

A month later came the summer homework: half a dozen words to be included in a story. I realised that mine just had to include our latest domestic crisis.

Which was that our kitchen ceiling came down on us, just two days after our daughter and her family returned from Uganda. Miraculously, it was the start of that spell of hot weather, we'd just finished eating in the garden and our grandchildren were upstairs having baths when the crack appeared.

Our crisis progressed much as the one described in "Chariots of Wire", although in our case what was revealed in the rafters was faded newspaper cuttings from the last century. These made me ponder what else might have been found in the early 1900s; and hence to the first Isle of Man TT Race (which really did have a cathartic moment at Devil's Elbow, including a hastily mended puncture).

129

The rafters behind our 1920s ceiling plaster (after cleaning!).

After I had completed my first homework entry, my wife challenged me to write another one, using the same six words. The challenge, met after a struggle, proved addictive. In the end I produced six stories, all of which are scattered through this book.

The challenge for you, dear reader, is to identify the other five stories; and the six words common to them all.

My final source of inspiration was new stories about established characters from earlier *Tales of Peril and Predicament*.

I needed one on the early life of George, the heroine of my *Cornish Conundrums*. I'd already documented her days before and during University: what might come next?

After a dismal start sketching her early career, I realised I had never covered George's meeting with future husband Mark Gilbert. How might that have happened? I tried; and at long last had an uncontrived silver lining.

Then there were my golfers, Greg and Laurie. They needed to widen their horizons: what if their golf course was used for serious filming? Or for a high-level reconciliation? Or even had a missing hole? Now I also had a black hole.

Lastly came Lauren Shaw, a rare black policewoman in Scarborough. Might she also perform in a play about racism?

By September the Ukraine conflict continued. What might have happened next to Anna? I hope you like the sequel.

Thanks to my wife, Marion, who has acted as my refiner and chief editor. Please send any comments to my website (below). Or put a one-line review on Amazon.

David Burnell   *website: davidburnell.info*
November 2022

Printed in Great Britain
by Amazon

24563666R00079